DUMP

Also by Bob Marshall-Andrews

The Palace of Wisdom

A Man Without Guilt

Off Message

Camille

ABOUT THE AUTHOR

Bob Marshall-Andrews is a writer and criminal silk based in London.

From 1997 to 2010 he was Labour MP for Medway. As a result of his relationship with New Labour, one magazine described him as 'the thorn in Tony Blair's Red Rose'. His political memoir *Off Message* was published by Profile in 2011. *Dump* is his fourth novel.

He lives in London and Pembrokeshire and is frequently in East Africa in his role as Chairman of the George Adamson Wildlife Trust.

Bob Marshall-Andrews

DUMP

A Novel

First published in the United Kingdom in 2017 by
Whitefox Publishing Ltd.
39 Roderick Road
London NW3 2NP

ISBN 978-1-911195-59-7

Also available as an ebook
ISBN 978-1-911195-58-0

Designed and typeset by K.DESIGN, Winscombe, Somerset
Cover design by James Nunn

Printed and bound by Clays Ltd, St Ives plc.

BOOK ONE

The Serole Lodge

2017.

CHAPTER 1

They had found the remains of Hector in thick undergrowth on the edge of the forest where it merged into the white sand on the shore of the lake. Moses took me there on the day of my return to the Serole Lodge.

'We find head over there,' he said, gesturing along the beach. 'Part of leg too, left leg I think. Rest of body we find here.' He pointed to a small clearing of flattened bush, branches still broken and torn as evidence of violent conflict. 'Balls torn off,' he continued, 'but we do not find them.'

I stared at him. 'The head had been cut from the body?'

'Not cut, no sign of panga, knife or saw – torn from the body. One eye missing. Also, several teeth.'

I continued to stare. 'This was the result of a fight?'

'Not fight, attack.'

I remembered Hector well. He was a big male, number three, after Ajax and Darwin. He was likely to be the next alpha male.

'Good God,' I said, 'when did this happen?'

'Three days ago. Two days after the others.'

'*The others?*'

'Two young subordinate males. Balthazar and Wilson. Same thing, much injury and damage. Heads off, balls off.'

'Another fight?'

'Not fight, attack.'

3

'Who did this, Moses? Leopards, hyena?'

Moses looked at me and then away into the forest and up to the mountains, now clearly visible in the morning sun. He shook his head and spoke a single word. 'Dump,' he said.

'*Dump!*'

'Yes, his name is Ronald but you call him Dump.'

'But Dump is dead. He has been dead for ten years. I killed him ten years ago.'

Moses continued to shake his head. 'He is not dead. He is out there.'

'But he had no family – even if he hadn't been killed, he was an outcast. He could not have survived.'

'He survived. He's out there with others.'

'Others? From the Serole troupe?'

'Not from the Serole troupe, not habituated. From the forest. They come from far. They are driven out by loggers, bad men, Chinese men drive them out.'

I was silent for a full minute, looking over the lake. Finally, I turned to Moses and said: 'How do you know it is Dump?'

Moses smiled for the first time. 'He leave his sign, his signal. You remember now, he leaves sign in both places. I show you.'

He crossed the clearing to an area where a tree had been uprooted and thrown back into the jungle.

'There,' he said, pointing with his stick.

I did not have to look too hard. A large pile of drying dung gave off a pungent smell. As Moses waved his stick, a cloud of flies rose up and then settled again. I found myself breathing deeply.

'Let us get away from here,' I said.

When we arrived back on the beach I became, once more, the academic. 'Where,' I said, 'are the bodies, the remains?'

Moses did not reply but pointed across the lake. He raised his eyebrows, anticipating my reaction.

'In the lake? They have been put in the lake?'

Moses nodded. 'All remains gone into the lake. Far, far out in weighted sack, water a thousand metres deep. They are gone.'

I found myself looking across the calm expanse of water. A stupid and futile search for floating heads. I turned back to Moses and realised that my old guide and friend was also staring out across the vast basin, Lake Tanganyika, containing seventeen per cent of the world's fresh water and the weighted remains of three chimpanzees. I asked the inevitable question.

'Does Edouard know about this?'

Moses nodded. 'He give the order. He tells us to throw into lake.'

'Does he know that you have told me?'

'I told him I would and he said nothing.'

'I will go and talk to him. But, Moses, tell me this, where is the Serole troupe? I have been here all day. I have been only a little way into the forest but it is silent. I have not seen or heard a single chimpanzee. Do you know where they are?'

'I think some of them hide but Ajax is around. Ajax, Regan, Gertrude, Priam, Horatio, they are still close but not happy. Not like they were. You will see.'

I walked with Moses back to the lodge. We trudged through the soft sand in silence. The buildings came into view. First Edouard's tented hut. I could see him outside on his veranda, inspecting the covering of thatch but conscious, I am sure, of our approach. The thatched roofs of the lodge and the beach huts beyond had not changed in the last ten years and memories stirred within me. The best years of my life.

As we drew closer, Edouard hailed me from the veranda. His French accent, I noticed, as always, was meticulously maintained.

'Arthur, come and have some coffee. I have just made it. It is Kenyan coffee and I have some fresh milk.'

Moses left me with a slight shrug and I climbed the steps to Edouard's house and office.

Edouard Deprès had lived in the Serole Lodge for twenty-five years. His wife, a Parisienne, had long ago departed and left Edouard to his intellectual passion (chimpanzees) and his candid preference for many assorted women. His latest mistress had gone to Dar es Salaam on the same boat which had carried me on my return journey across the lake. His residence, although a little more spacious and grand, in fact closely resembled the eight guest tents which were set out at intervals of forty metres along the side of the lake. They were separated from the water by barely thirty metres of white sand. Their construction was near-identical although they varied in size. All of them were large canvas tents with wooden walls surrounding the interior to a height of approximately one metre. Inside they were divided into one, two or three bedroom areas with showers and bathrooms attached. All the rooms contained Swahili beds and furniture and their hardwood floors were polished to a low gloss which glowed in the electric lights powered by solar panels. A generator discreetly housed behind the kitchen and the staff quarters was invisible in the jungle itself. Brochures described the Serole Lodge as 'jungle luxury', which was not far from the truth. The lodge building itself was a similar thatched construction, approximately thirty metres long, twenty metres wide and six metres high. It was divided into two floors. On

6

the ground, or beach level, there was a large dining room, a bar and sitting areas. Above, surrounding a central atrium, was a library which consisted partly of academic works relating to chimpanzees and other forest animals, many of them of considerable age, reflecting a colonial past. Most of these books were in English, German or French. More recent titles included Japanese, Chinese and Italian. Otherwise the library contained several hundred volumes, mainly paperback, which had been left over a period of forty years by departing guests. It was in this area that I had spent much of my ten years at Serole, happily engrossed in the study of chimpanzees. I had been joined by successive research students. They culminated with Claire Watkins, to whom I was now married and who was expected to join me the following day after three months in Uganda. Her imminent arrival was the first topic of conversation between Edouard and myself as I settled into a chair on his veranda and accepted a large mug of black coffee.

'So, we are expecting Claire on tomorrow's boat,' said Edouard. 'She is coming in with our new guests.'

'She is,' I said. 'Do we have many?'

Edouard made a show of counting on his fingers. 'Eleven,' he concluded, 'including Claire herself. You and I will make the number to thirteen. I have hardly had time to speak to you since you arrived. Are you happy in your old house?'

'It is fine as always, Edouard. Indeed, you have made a number of significant improvements.'

'And are you and Claire happy at Oxford? They have given you a Chair, I hear. *Professor* Arthur Welbourne indeed, and richly deserved. We have a copy of *The Prototype Primate* in the library.'

7

'I sent it to you when it was published.'

'So you did. Did it sell well?'

'As well as any book of primate research. We are all overshadowed by Goodall and Fossey. But, yes, thank you, we are very happy. I am, however,' I continued, setting my coffee cup down on the table, 'very concerned at what I have just learnt.'

'Yes, I saw you talking to Moses as you walked along the beach. I suppose he has been regaling you with his theories about Dump, apparently risen from the dead.'

'He also told me about Hector and the two other deaths.'

'Ah, yes, a particularly nasty outbreak of fighting. Ajax is getting on, I'm afraid. There is bound to be trouble before they decide on the next alpha male. Ajax has, after all, been around for over ten years.'

'It did not seem hierarchical to me. The degree of violence is unique and Hector's body was dismembered.'

'Hardly dismembered. His head had come off, that's all.'

'And part of his leg and his testicles.'

'Really? I was not aware of those details. Yes, it was rather nasty but it is the kind of thing that happens over the years.'

I was staring at him in disbelief. 'Edouard,' I said, 'this happened three days ago and was the third such attack. Did you not see it for yourself?'

'Well, Moses told me about it, of course, and described it in some detail but I have been very busy, Arthur, very busy, and we are about to have one of the most important, *and lucrative*, tours we have ever had. I am afraid that I probably didn't give it the attention that I should have.'

'Moses said that you went and inspected the remains yourself.'

'Did he? Well, I suppose I must have done. Yes, I did as a

matter of fact and you are quite right, it was very nasty, but the important thing was to clear it up.'

'Edouard, I repeat I simply do not believe I am hearing this. I studied this troupe for ten years and only once encountered an attack even remotely as violent. Now there are three dead chimps. Three. Those remains should have been preserved for study. At the very least this represents an entirely new pattern of behaviour by an individual or, worse still, a group. I understand that the bodies have been thrown into the lake in weighted sacks. Is that true?'

Edouard stared at me from across his mug of coffee and then transferred his gaze to a large framed picture of Dian Fossey and an enormous male gorilla, apparently enjoying a shared joke.

'Arthur, I do not accept this at all. Perhaps you are right that the remains should have been preserved but we have no adequate storage. I don't know where you think we should have kept them. All the chest freezers are packed as we have a full complement of guests. In this heat, the . . . remains would become a health hazard within hours. In case you are not aware, I have Jolyon Downside, the English actor, coming next week. There is also an important party from America. Swift action had to be taken and the lake was the best option.'

'Let us set that aside for the moment. What about Dump?'

'A theory of Moses's, nothing more. We all know that Dump was a bit of a problem ten years ago but he is dead, Arthur, dead. You above all people should know, because you killed him, several blows with a machete if memory serves. We all know why you did it: he was in the course of a savage attack on Ajax, and there is little point in rehearsing it. You broke the rules, Arthur, which is why we have not seen you for ten years. But you did it. If I remember rightly, you practically cut his head off.'

'The body was never found.'

'No, it was not, but he was tracked and the quantity of blood alone would have ensured he could not survive – and also he was expelled from the troupe. No one knows better than you that chimpanzees cannot live outside their troupe.'

'There are other troupes.'

Edouard made a gesture of extreme impatience. 'Other troupes? Of course there are other troupes. There are seven hundred chimpanzees out there. But fully grown males are never accepted into other troupes. You know that better than anyone else. They will be ostracised and killed, particularly if they are like Dump.'

Under this onslaught I could feel myself losing my temper. 'But that's just it. No normal chimpanzee could survive but Dump is, was, not normal.'

It was Edouard's turn to express disbelief. 'Arthur,' he said learning forward. 'What exactly do you mean, *not normal*?'

'He was incredibly violent. He bullied and abused his mother.'

'Yes, yes, that was unfortunate but the chimpanzees sorted it out in their own way. Without putting too fine a point on it, he was rather an unpleasant ape but what do you mean by *not normal*?'

'He was demented, deranged; he was a classic psychopath. He displayed no guilt, no empathy.'

Edouard held up his hands. He was beginning to smile. 'Arthur, you know perfectly well as an academic you simply cannot start using those terms. Chimpanzees do not have empathy any more than they have God. They do not have a Christian Hellenic guilt complex any more than a weasel. They might share ninety-eight per cent of our DNA but somewhere in that other two per cent is the whole world of science and literature, philosophy, empathy, religion and, above all, guilt. No chimpanzee feels guilty because they are missing the two per cent which gives us guilt. You may say, if you were being cynical, the bit that buggers us up. They do not have norms, they have habits. They do not have social guilt; they have survival instincts. Dump may well have been a supreme example of the survival instinct but that's what he was. Dump was normal. Because he's normal he cannot be a psychopath or psychotic or neurotic or anything else. Because he's a normal chimp he will not react to the psychiatrist, psychologist, Freudian, Jungian or anyone else. Because he's normal he will not react to counselling. And, most of all, because he's normal he's dead. Now, would you like some more coffee?'

Edouard rose and five minutes later reappeared with two mugs. 'There we are,' he said, 'now let's forget about it.'

I took a long sip of my coffee, blew across the top, placed the cup on the table and said very quietly, 'No, Edouard, I am afraid not. I hear what you say and, of course, you make some sense but normal, psychotic, psychopathic or not, the violence described by Moses is extreme. Furthermore, it could not have been committed by one animal. Without going into detail, to tear the head from the body requires teamwork, likewise the leg or part of it. Dump or no Dump, something is going very wrong here. You cannot have, simply cannot have, twelve guests in this lodge at this time. Until we have resolved this thing this visit must be cancelled or postponed.'

Edouard surveyed me across his coffee cup in turn and his eyes smouldered with something close to desperation. 'No,

Arthur, definitely not. Please do not come back here, after ten years, and make complications. There will be no cancellations and no postponements. Let me tell you something, old friend. This lodge, this wonderful place which has been my home for twenty-five years, is in trouble. This piece of paradise, this outpost of liberal civilisation, research and academia, is, to employ the topical vernacular, in deep shit. Let me tell you what has happened. First, the tourist trade has slumped. This is due to terrorism and Ebola. It is also linked to the American State Department. The Ebola outbreak in West Africa is six thousand kilometres from Lake Tanganyika. You are more likely to catch Ebola in New York than you are in Dar es Salaam. That has no effect on the American State Department, who operate on the basis that in Africa we are all black and diseased. Also, there have been terrorist attacks in Kenya. Not many, but there have been. There have been fewer, incidentally, than in France or in Belgium or even in the jolly old United Kingdom. There have been infinitely fewer deaths by gunfire in the whole of East Africa than in the United States. That does not stop the American State Department putting a blanket warning on their precious citizens going to Africa full stop. The result has been a disaster.'

He drank some coffee and continued, 'In addition to that, European universities are engaging in a massive cutback in research. Not commercial research, that is where the money is going, but in soft research, if you like civilised research, research into humanity and its relations with the natural world. All of that has been savagely cut. Your own doctorate would not now have been possible. As a result, we are in deep financial trouble. Putting it bluntly, if we cancel this week's bookings we are finished. That is particularly so as these bookings are the most valuable that we have had all season. That may mean something to you, Arthur. Commercial failure may be one thing but the future of this piece of civilisation, this outpost of liberal learning and research, is in deadly danger. So, now you see why this week's visit will not be cancelled.'

There was a long silence before I said, 'But what if . . .'

'What if? What if? What do you mean? What if there is an accident? What if there is a violent event? Arthur, the risk of such an event is tiny, microscopic, and you know that to be so. You know because you are an immensely distinguished academic and an expert in chimpanzee behaviour. You know that chimpanzees do not attack people. Chimpanzees are permanently in danger from people, from disease and from the destruction of their homes. They have every right and excuse to attack people but *they do not do it*. Chimpanzees do not fight back. So our guests may not actually see a chimpanzee, but they will certainly not be harmed by a chimpanzee.'

Another long pause ensued before I said, 'Who's coming? Who is on the guest list?'

'I was hoping you would ask that. Firstly, we have Jolyon Downside and Cindy Applebloom. Have you heard of her?'

'Yes.'

'Well, she has recently been starring with him in a film called *Roger*. Roger is a chimpanzee who goes to Oxford to obtain a DPhil. It will come out in two weeks' time and they are on a publicity exercise for which they have paid much, much money. Next comes Mr Hiram Sidewinder III and his family, which consists of four other Sidewinders. You have heard of him?'

'Isn't he a dentist?'

13

'Yes, indeed, he is a dentist, a very, very wealthy dentist from Tennessee. He is also a hunter and has been with his family slaughtering animals in the Selous game reserve. All properly licensed and, I suspect, deeply corrupt. Anyway, the Sidewinders want a little break from the massacre of wildlife and so are coming here for four days to enjoy some R and R on Lake Tanganyika with the prospect of seeing the odd chimpanzee. For this privilege they have paid much, *much money*. They have paid at hunters' rate, which is approximately triple what tourists pay. Then we have some normal guests, two ladies from Britain, the Bellingham sisters, and a Chinese researcher from an incomprehensible university. They are paying ordinary rates but the total makes for an extraordinary sum. Now, Arthur, do you see how serious this is?'

It was compelling and, of course, he was right. Chimpanzees did not attack human beings. According to all usual laws the party was safe. Also, I confess, I was longing for the arrival of Claire, whom I had not seen for many weeks. Edouard sensed that I was weakening and played a final card.

'There is one matter otherwise unconnected which you may find persuasive. There has been substantial illegal logging in the National Park. You cannot see it or hear it from here but I have seen it from the top of that mountain. It is in the far distance but it daily grows. It is, of course, corrupt. The Chinese have paid vast sums for the privilege of destroying paradise. It makes us more important. If we go, if we disappear, there will be nothing left to stop them. No focus of attention, no one to tell the world what is happening. This wonderful park will surely disappear and with it the chimpanzees, normal or otherwise. That's another reason why we want the Chinese researcher, whatever his name is. We have got to get the little buggers on our side.'

I stood up, finished my coffee and set down the mug. 'You are a persuasive old devil, Edouard. It must be the French accent. You are not right but you are probably less wrong than me. I will keep my counsel. If you will let us, Claire and I will help you with your actors and your dentist and hope that Dump is dead.'

CHAPTER 2

I stood with Edouard on the beach and watched the boat round the headland. As usual, the guests could be seen lining the side, anxious for a first glimpse of the lodge and the thatched cottages lining the white beach and framed by the mountains and the forests behind. It was a conventional paradise but impressive nonetheless. I could see Claire standing at the prow alone, supporting herself against the balustrade. She looked magnificent.

As the boat grounded, steps were lowered and she was the first to come ashore. Eagerly I embraced her. I said, 'Darling, you look magnificent.' She said, 'Christ, I need a drink.'

We left Edouard and the staff to welcome the guests, dispense chilled tea, allocate the rooms and disperse the luggage. We entered the shade of the lodge and Claire sat at the bar while I prepared two strong gin and tonics.

I leaned on the bar and said, 'Well, how was the journey?'

She downed a good slug of the liquor, set her glass on the bar and said, 'God, what a bunch. Do you know who they are?'

'I've seen the guest list and Edouard has described them in some detail. He is particularly anxious about Mr Sidewinder, our multimillionaire dentist from Memphis.'

'And well he might be. Sidewinder is now a fully-fledged international celebrity or global criminal, take your pick. He is a hunter. The whole family are hunters. He is Hiram

Sidewinder *the third*, so get it right. In addition to him there is Mrs Sidewinder (*the first*, I suspect), two twins, all-American boys aged about eighteen, and a ghastly little twelve-year-old called Violet. They have all spent two weeks happily decimating wildlife down in the Selous.'

'They won't be the first hunters we have had here.'

'Maybe not, but he succeeded in shooting a giraffe without a permit. There's a picture gone viral on the social networks with his foot on the animal's neck. It's in all the papers. "The dental killer from Memphis", "The Tennessee tooth butcher", etc., etc.'

'Oh God,' I said, reaching for the gin bottle and a refill. 'Christ, do they know he's coming here, the press I mean?'

'Not yet.'

'We had better keep it that way, radio silence and all that.'

'It's not that simple. We've got two English sisters, spinsters of indeterminate age who are connected with some donkey charity. Donkeys, camels, mules, beasts of burden – anyway they have read the giraffe stuff and obviously regard Sidewinder as some kind of mass murderer. They haven't said anything openly but I've heard them muttering.'

'Well, they are not likely to tell the world's press. "Donkey Do-gooders on Ape Holiday with Memphis Killer Dentist"? That wouldn't look too good.'

Claire finished her drink and held out the empty glass.

'There is another problem. We've also got Jolyon Downside and Cindy Applebloom. The Bellingham sisters were quite overcome when they saw him. One of them actually asked him to autograph her donkey brochure. She said his role as John Trotter in the *Trotter Files* was the best thing she had ever seen on television. At least it is good news for the Bellinghams, but the bad news is the reason that they are here. You may not know this but they are starring in a film about a chimpanzee who goes to Oxford and gets a DPhil in business studies or something. They are out here with a photographer to take publicity pictures with real chimps. It is due to be released in two weeks so there is a substantial risk that we might have Hiram Sidewinder III in the background. I have mentioned this to the photographer, nice chap called Boxe, but it is a worry we could do without.'

I nodded as I refilled her drink. 'As a matter of fact I did know about *Roger*. The director wrote to me and asked me if I would advise on chimpanzee behaviour. They sent me an early cut of the film and an appalling script. Of course, I refused.'

'You didn't tell me this. Anyway, apparently they brought an advance DVD of the movie.'

'Oh God. Is that all?'

'That just about makes up the party, apart from a Chinese researcher from an unpronounceable university. So far he has said nothing; he sits in the boat making notes. So that's my news. How about the chimps?'

'Haven't seen any.'

'*None?*'

'No. I have been well into the forest, calling for them. It's very strange but I think it may be connected to something much worse.'

'Worse?'

I took a deep breath, looked straight into her eyes and said, 'Do you remember Dump?'

'Dump? Dump? *Ronald Dump*, the psychopathic male? Of course I remember Dump, he's dead. You killed him.'

'I think, unhappily, that that may not be the case. I'll tell you about it. Cheers.'

CHAPTER 3

The entire party assembled in the library area above the dining room at four thirty. In the lodge brochure this gathering was described as the briefing meeting. The weather was hot and had turned humid. The Sidewinder family wore shorts and T-shirts. The Bellinghams wore near-identical print dresses and sensible trainers. Jolyon Downside, Cindy Applebloom and John Boxe wore suits of designer khaki. The Chinese researcher appeared in jeans and a shirt. Claire, myself, Edouard and the three guides, Moses, Benedict and Boniface, wore the lodge uniform, monogrammed grey bush suits and safari boots. There was a smattering of light conversation and some intermingling. Hiram Sidewinder politely offered a tray of biscuits to the Bellingham sisters, who refused. At four thirty-five, Edouard gave a small cough, silence descended and he began.

'Good afternoon and welcome. I hope you have all had a pleasant boat trip and by now you will all have been introduced to each other.' This was greeted with universal nods. The Bellingham sisters, I noticed, nodded particularly energetically in the direction of Jolyon Downside, who returned the gesture with a smile of the utmost charm.

Edouard continued. 'May I begin with a few ground rules? In the next four days you will, I hope, come into close contact with the chimpanzees. We have, around the lodge, a large troupe or family of some sixty individuals. They are all habituated, they are quite used to humans. They may come very close. They may even push or pull you in a friendly fashion. They may also show off in various ways. The males, in particular, may engage in a false charge. Do not be alarmed. They will stop within a few feet, they may gesticulate and will then simply walk off. You have been provided with surgical masks which attach over the ears. It is a golden rule that you should always wear these masks when in the vicinity of the chimpanzees. This is for their protection and not yours.

'You will find that in many ways they are remarkably human. They are our nearest ancestors and share ninety-eight per cent of our DNA. Cameras and mobile phones are, of course, permitted but keep a firm hold on them. Chimpanzees, like us, are fond of gadgets and are attracted to them. Do not carry hiking sticks or pointed sticks of any kind. They may be treated as offensive weapons. If you require a stick for walking purposes, ask your guide and he will give you one cut from the forest itself.

'The Serole troupe have lived around the lodge now for nearly half a century. They are well known to us and are our friends. Over there, on the wall, you will see a family tree setting out the present troupe. At the top there is the alpha male, Ajax, and beneath him a number of the subordinate males, Hector, Priam, Darwin, Horatio, Brutus, Carter and Achilles. On the right-hand side are the females, the oldest and most senior of whom are Gertrude and Regan. There are then a number of subordinate females. Below these individuals there are approximately forty junior members of the troupe. You will notice that most of them are directly connected to a female parent. However, none is linked to any specific male. The reason for this is simple.

Chimpanzees are extremely promiscuous. When the females come into season they will mate with many males over a very short period of time. It is thus impossible in the absence of detailed DNA analysis to ascribe a baby to any particular father. The mating act of a chimpanzee is a very cursory business. It lasts approximately five seconds.'

'Not much in the way of foreplay?' said Hiram Sidewinder loudly to his wife.

'No, it is not a romantic scene, I'm afraid,' Edouard continued. 'What is often mistaken for chimp heavy petting is, in fact, the mutual removing of lice and insects from each other's fur. As to where and when we will meet the chimpanzees, it is difficult to say. Frequently members of the Serole group come into the lodge grounds itself and may come into the immediate neighbourhood of your huts. Do not be alarmed; as I say, they are our friends. That said, rather unusually, there have been no chimpanzees in the lodge grounds for over a week. This is uncommon but not unique. It means that we will have to track them into the forest. Moses will take out a party tomorrow morning for anyone who wishes to go on a day's trek. You are, of course, perfectly welcome to remain in the lodge or on the beach. Often some rest and relaxation is welcome on your first day. In order to prepare your food could I please have a show of hands of those who wish to trek and those who wish to stay in the lodge. Trekkers please.'

The hands of the Bellingham sisters rose immediately. The Sidewinders conferred among themselves and indicated that they would remain at the lodge. Jolyon Downside and Cindy Applebloom shook their heads and Yojo Bo Fang remained impassive.

'Right then,' said Edouard, 'that looks like just you ladies to go out with Moses tomorrow. He normally starts at about half past ten and you will return to the lodge at about four o'clock. Now, finally, we have, I understand, a treat in store. Jolyon and Cindy have recently made a film which some of you may have heard of. It is called *Roger* and concerns a chimpanzee who goes to Oxford University. I am told it is very moving. Jolyon has brought a copy with him and I suggest that we should all assemble here again at half past five, prior to dinner which will be at seven thirty. Before that takes place we may view *Roger* on the screen over there, which is specifically designed for the playing of DVDs.'

As the party dispersed Edouard intercepted us at the bar. 'I don't suppose you will be coming to watch *Roger*?'

I smiled and shook my head. 'Once is enough,' I said. 'We will see you here when it is all over.'

CHAPTER 4

We returned to the bar early. From the library we heard the concluding theme music from *Roger* rising to a climax. I recognised Beethoven's Emperor Concerto.

When the party descended the stairs it was led by Claudia Bellingham, dabbing her eyes with a large embroidered handkerchief. Immediately behind her, her sister maintained a face of rigorous self-control. 'My God,' she muttered. 'What a film!'

The Sidewinder family came down next. Hiram Sidewinder clutched an empty whisky glass, shaking his head slowly from side to side, signifying a man deeply moved. Jolyon Downside and Cindy Applebloom brought up the rear, adopting the noble bearing of deserved celebrity. Edouard Deprès came down last carrying the acclaimed DVD. When they reached the table he handed it to Jolyon Downside with obvious reverence.

'There you are, Jolyon. You had better take good care of that.'

Yojo Bo Fang, the Chinese researcher, and John Boxe, the photographer, had decided not to join the party at dinner and they remained in the library upstairs where they would be served a separate meal. Edouard took charge fussing over the placement and dispensing drinks, fruit juice for the Bellinghams, beer for Josh and Randy Sidewinder, another large whisky for Hiram Sidewinder and white wine for everybody else. The first course, prawn cocktail, was already on the table, together with crusty bread and small pots of butter. Jolyon Downside, as befitted the moment, was placed at the head of the table, Cindy Applebloom on his right.

Winnie Sidewinder began with the inevitable: 'Oh my God, what a film, what a film.'

'Don't,' said Claudia Bellingham, 'you'll start me off again.'

Undeterred, Winnie Sidewinder continued. 'But what an ending, *what* an ending! The way he walked down the street wearing his gown, carrying his mortarboard, standing out magnificently, an ape in a sea of humans.'

'Proud but humble,' said Hiram Sidewinder.

To his immediate right Claudia Bellingham was again dabbing her eyes with the embroidered handkerchief.

'What I really liked,' said Randy Sidewinder, sipping his beer. 'What I really liked is the fact that you had already seen the lorry, that supermarket lorry, being loaded. What was the supermarket again?'

Claudia Bellingham spoke through a sob. 'Sainsbury's.'

'Yeah, yeah, Sainsbury's. And you know, without being told, that's going to be the lorry that finishes him off. That's going to be his, what's the word?'

'Nemesis,' said Pat Bellingham. 'Nemesis.'

'Yeah, that's right. His nemesis. When you see the lorry coming round that building, that old round building with the old heads outside it. What's it called?'

'Arthur will know,' said Edouard.

'The Sheldonian,' I said shortly.

'Sure, sure, the Shelbonian. Just as Roger passes the gates and then you see the driver, on his mobile phone talking about bananas, I like that.'

Claudia Bellingham let out a muffled sob.

Josh Sidewinder joined his brother's account. 'Yeah, and you never see the collision. I like that, I like that.'

'You just hear it,' said his mother.

'Yeah, you hear it. Just a muffled thud and a scream but you don't see it. All you see is the mortarboard sailing through the air.'

'And then,' said Hiram Sidewinder, 'it lands on one of those heads around the Shelbonian. Who is it? Nelson, Churchill?'

'Augustus,' I said quietly. 'The Roman emperor.'

'Yeah, Augustus. Mortarboard lands on his head. I really liked that. I thought it was really clever.'

Pat Bellingham turned to Jolyon Downside and Cindy Applebloom. 'And then you two come on the scene driving the family car that still has Roger's baby seat in the back and you just find him lying on the pavement.'

Jolyon Downside smiled a wise and solemn smile. 'But not dead.'

'No, not dead, not dead,' said Winnie Sidewinder, 'but speechless and pointing, just pointing that chimpanzee's finger just like in *ET*. Pointing upwards and then you see the camera swing to show you the mortarboard.'

Randy Sidewinder unnecessarily intervened. 'Yeah, yeah, he's just saying, or not saying, "I want my mortarboard."'

'And then I love the way that it is the Sainsbury's driver,' said Winnie Sidewinder, 'who climbs up the railings and gets the mortarboard, which he carries down and gives to you.'

'No,' said Cindy Applebloom. 'He doesn't give it to Jolyon, he gives it to me. There is a great shot where I just look at the mortarboard with Roger dying behind me, still pointing. And the audience thinks: *Will she give it to him in time?* Then I turn slowly and give it to Jolyon.'

'Right,' said Hiram Sidewinder. 'You give it to Jolyon and he, very slowly, gives it to Roger, who takes it in one hand and attempts to jam it on his head before he dies.'

In the ensuing silence Claudia Bellingham emitted a loud sob.

'What a movie,' said Hiram Sidewinder, 'what an ending.'

Silence ensued before Edouard unwisely turned to me. 'You've seen it before, Arthur, haven't you?'

'Unwillingly,' I answered. 'Yes, they sent it to me unsolicited, asking me to advise on chimpanzee behaviour.'

'And did you advise?'

'No, I did not. I sent it back.'

'So, what did you think of it? You have a DPhil from Oxford as well. So what did you think?'

I was trapped and a little drunk. I felt Claire kick me gently under the table. All eyes were upon me, expecting profundity. I took the line of least resistance.

'You don't wear mortarboards at Oxford for higher degrees.'

After a prolonged pause Hiram Sidewinder addressed Jolyon Downside. 'Is that right, Jolyon? Is that right?'

Jolyon Downside smiled a smile of utter condescension. 'I am sorry; I really don't know. I went to RADA myself, the Royal Academy of Dramatic Art. We certainly didn't wear mortarboards there, or get doctorates.'

The guests laughed politely and Hiram Sidewinder added: 'Well, I'm sure that doesn't matter very much. Dramatic licence and all that. It is art that matters, art and the effect on the human mind. Isn't that right, Claudia?'

Claudia Bellingham emitted a further sniff, which was taken

as a signal to begin the prawn cocktail. As we commenced eating Claire looked at me, raised an eyebrow and shrugged. It was an articulate gesture. 'Let us hope,' she murmured, 'that we have heard the last of Roger and his doctorate.'

It was not to be. As the starters were cleared away and the main course, red snapper, chips and salad, was served, Randy Sidewinder returned to the film.

'You know something,' he said, addressing Jolyon Downside. 'The most moving moment for me, I don't know about you but certainly for me, was the interview that Roger had with the university rugby coach.'

Jolyon Downside smiled in partial acquiescence and beside him Cindy Applebloom nodded energetically.

'Yes, yes. I liked that too, even though neither of us were actually in that scene.'

'I know,' Randy continued, 'but it was the way that the coach explained so, so gently that Roger could not be considered for the university side in the match against Cambridge.'

'The Varsity match,' said Jolyon Downside.

'Yeah, the Varsity match. That he would be unable to get his colours. What's it called? A "Blue"? You could see the pain in his face. It was beautifully done, beautiful.'

'I liked the way,' said Winnie Sidewinder, 'that at that point, when he got the news, he reverted and started to gibber in chimpanzee. *Duk, duk, duk, duk.*'

'And then the coach,' said Randy Sidewinder, 'embraced him and just held him. You could see at that point he was crying. The coach, I mean. And then the coach explained that he would have selected him but the Cambridge side had objected to playing against an "ape" and you saw the look of rejection in his eyes.'

'Discrimination!' said Winnie Sidewinder.

'I know how he felt,' said Hiram Sidewinder. 'When I was dropped from my freshman side at college it was the worst thing that had ever happened in my life and I did exactly what Roger did. I got drunk. I liked the way that he went to the college bar and stole a bottle of whisky, took it up to his room and drank it staring out of his window across the roofs of Oxford.'

'And then the way,' said Josh Sidewinder, 'that he picked up his thesis and you could feel yourself saying "Oh no, oh no," then he had another glass of whisky and picked up his thesis again, the size of a telephone directory, held it in both hands and then he looked straight at the camera, you remember that?'

'Oh yes,' said Winnie Sidewinder, 'a look of total pain.'

'And then he just ripped it up, tore it apart, and then again and again. It was terrible.'

After a short pause, Pat Bellingham addressed herself to Jolyon Downside. 'What do you suppose,' she asked, 'that the film is telling us? That scene, what is it saying?'

Jolyon Downside glanced briefly at Cindy Applebloom before leaning forward with intent. 'I spoke to the director. As you know, it was a Robert Bellbottom film. I said: "Robert, what does this scene mean? What does it tell us about the relationship between man and beast? Consciousness of failure, of discrimination?" And he said to me, "Well, it tells you that it takes an ape to tear up a thesis the size of a telephone directory." And that was it. Pure atavistic brute strength. But then I particularly liked the way he opened his window above the quad and slowly let the severed pages float into the night like falling snow until they covered the entire quad.'

'It was lucky,' said Pat Bellingham, 'that his tutor had kept a copy.'

'Yeah, that's right,' said Hiram Sidewinder; 'if he hadn't kept a copy then Roger would never have got his degree.'

'And never have died,' said Claudia Bellingham.

'Oh hell,' said Randy Sidewinder, 'you just can't say that, those "what ifs" in movies. He certainly would have died, he may not have been hit by a Sainsbury's truck outside the Shelbonian but he would have died somehow. But anyway,' he continued, turning to address me. 'So what do you think, Dr Welbourne? You've been very quiet. What did you think of that scene, the rugby scene?'

Apart from my observations on mortarboards, I had maintained a dedicated silence. I had also consumed the best part of a bottle of wine. Ignoring Claire's second kick under the table, I addressed myself to Jolyon Downside.

'I am sorry to say,' I said, 'that I thought it was painful drivel.'

Hiram Sidewinder said: 'Drivel? What the hell's drivel?'

'Rubbish,' I replied, 'worse than rubbish. Patronising, anthropomorphic rubbish.'

I saw Jolyon Downside scowl before Randy Sidewinder said: 'That's a very hard judgement on such a beautiful and original scene. Why do you say that?'

'Well, to start with, chimpanzees could not play rugby. By any kinetic measure they are three times stronger than human beings. Let loose on a rugby field, even assuming they could be trained, they would probably kill most of the opposing side before half-time, entirely unintentionally. In my view, for what it is worth, Cambridge were absolutely right to refuse to play. As a matter of interest, allowing the pages to fall like snow is a direct crib from Bergman. The one part that makes sense is that a chimpanzee could undoubtedly tear up a telephone directory, if such things still existed.'

From the other end of the table, Hiram Sidewinder gave a snort of derision. 'Oh come on, come on. This is not a serious movie. This is not intended to be a serious movie. This isn't about prison or war, for Christ's sake. This is just about an ape getting a degree.'

Ignoring Claire's third kick under the table, I persevered. 'I wish I could agree with you. Unhappily this is a serious film for three reasons. Firstly, it is seriously designed to make money. Secondly, it peddles populist rubbish about genetic modification and, thirdly, it is patronisingly anthropomorphic. While pretending to show that a genetically modified ape is as good as we are, it demonstrates precisely the reverse, that chimpanzees are inferior primates. The fact is they have evolved complex patterns of behaviour, in families and hierarchies, living by their own codes of fairness and justice. They have sophisticated means of communication and, when left alone in the wild, enjoy generally peaceful relations with other groups, or, if you will, with other nations. All of that appears to be completely ignored in favour of the superiority of Oxford and a plug for Sainsbury's home delivery.'

Aware of a fourth painful kick, I decided enough was enough. I raised my wine glass and, in an attempt at jocularity, said: 'Cheers, here's to Roger.'

The renewed silence was interrupted by Jolyon Downside, who affected a display of good humour. 'Well, Arthur,' he said, 'I can see why you didn't agree to consult on the film but we shall all look forward to reading your favourable reviews.'

A little polite laughter followed, which was immediately silenced by a noise from the surrounding forest, now dark and barely moonlit beyond the boundaries of the beach. It began as a chattering cry then rose into a single scream which grew in volume and pitch until, after fully half a minute, it stopped abruptly. Within seconds it was repeated from a location well to the south and then again, from a greater distance higher in the mountains. No sooner had the first three calls receded than they were repeated along the shoreline, then finally disappeared into the silence.

'Christ,' said Hiram Sidewinder. 'What the hell was that noise?'

Edouard and I looked at each other across the candles before he said: 'That's the chimpanzees. They are obviously putting on a show. They are quite close so we should be lucky and see them tomorrow.'

'Well,' said Hiram Sidewinder, 'unless they come right into the camp they won't be seen by me. I'm taking tomorrow as a day of R and R by the lake.'

Jolyon Downside nodded in agreement. 'We came on the overnight flight from London. A day of rest would be good.'

'That's fine,' said Edouard. 'I will make arrangements. Now enjoy the rest of your meal. I must go to see the staff and the kitchen.'

As he walked past me and Claire, he gestured to us both. We rose and followed him on to the beach.

'What,' I said quietly, 'did you make of that sound?'

Edouard looked straight at me. 'I have heard it twice before. Both occasions were last week. They sound like hunting cries, only longer.' He hesitated for a moment before adding: 'They appear to be in chorus.'

'That is what I thought,' I said. 'I have never heard of it before. There appeared to be an orchestration.'

Later Claire and I sat together on the veranda of our hut. There was silence in the forest and the gentle waves of the lake broke evenly on the sand. A freshening wind was the only sign of the threatened storm. We had a bottle of wine between us and Claire refilled our glasses before she said: 'What are you going to do? You're worried, aren't you?'

'Of course,' I replied, 'but there is nothing to be done immediately.'

'Those calls, the hunting calls, they are not normal, are they?'

'No, I don't think so, but then I have been out of the field for ten years and I don't know everything.'

Claire smiled in the darkness. 'But you do have a DPhil, the size of a telephone directory.'

I smiled back. 'And just about as useful.'

CHAPTER 5

Breakfast began at seven thirty. By eight o'clock, the majority of the party had assembled and were seated around the table. Edouard sat at the head with one Bellingham sister on either side. The Sidewinder twins sat together facing the lake with their parents. Violet Sidewinder had remained in bed, as had Jolyon Downside and Cindy Applebloom. The latter had apparently ordered a continental breakfast, which was carried across the beach by Coleridge, one of the two serving staff. Claire and I occupied the far end of the table. Of Yojo Bo Fang there was no sign. Erasmus was introduced as the chief waiter and barman and took orders for breakfast. Poached eggs on toast for the Bellingham sisters, a full English breakfast for the Sidewinders and John Boxe, fruit and porridge for myself and Claire. Edouard drank coffee and ordered two slices of toast and marmalade.

'So, you ladies,' said Hiram Sidewinder, 'you ladies are vegetarians.'

Claudia Bellingham glanced at her sister and said, 'Yes, we have been vegetarians all our lives.'

'But not vegan,' said Winnie Sidewinder; 'eggs is okay, right?'

Pat Bellingham answered, 'No, we are not vegan. No animal has died to produce a poached egg.'

'Hell, that's right,' said Hiram Sidewinder, 'there's that old thing about bacon and eggs. The pig is committed, the hen contributes. Ain't that right?'

'Just so,' said Pat Bellingham.

'For myself,' continued Hiram Sidewinder, failing to observe a warning look from his wife, 'for myself, I take an ethical position on this. I think if you are going to shoot animals then you have got to eat them. Not every single one you shoot, of course, just the edible ones. I'm not advocating eating cats, lions, leopards, which are for trophies only. I've two lions on the wall of my waiting room; magnificent teeth. But if you can eat it, eat it. Just to kill it without eating it, hell, that's wrong. Hell, I shot a hippopotamus in 19—'

Winnie Sidewinder cut across her husband. 'But you ladies have a professional interest in animals, do you not?'

Claudia Bellingham opened her eyes, which had been tightly closed, and directed them towards Winnie Sidewinder. 'Yes, we are interested in donkeys. Mules too, although there are far fewer of them. We work for International Donkey Rescue, as volunteers of course.'

'International Donkey Rescue?' said Randy Sidewinder. 'I've seen an advert for that in one of my magazines. What exactly do you do, internationally I mean?'

'We operate donkey sanctuaries,' said Pat Bellingham. 'We have two in Tanzania, one in Dar es Salaam and one in Arusha.'

'And how many donkeys do you have in these sanctuaries?' asked Josh Sidewinder.

'In all we have two thousand.'

Josh Sidewinder whistled while Randy Sidewinder continued, 'And how do they get into the sanctuary? Do they just wander in? Do you advertise or is it by word of mouth?'

Claudia Bellingham's tone became a little acid. 'No, they do not just wander in. By the time they get there, many of them cannot even walk and a lot of them couldn't see to get in either. We have volunteers who go and find them when they are no longer of any use to their owners, to whom we pay a small sum of money.'

Winnie Sidewinder nodded sympathetically before her husband said, 'I've never shot a donkey. To tell you the truth, I've never even thought about shooting one.'

'Shot horses,' said Randy Sidewinder.

'Hell, horses, yah. We shot hundreds of wild horses down in Arizona. They've got too many goddamn horses down there so you need to take them out.'

'How very distressing,' said Claudia Bellingham.

'Hell, no, they don't even know what hits 'em. But you could say we are both in the animal conservation business. That's what I say. The best way to conserve animals is to kill them.'

'Would you like some more toast?' said Edouard to Pat Bellingham. 'Marmalade?'

Hiram Sidewinder went on. 'You've got to put a value on the animals, especially here in Africa with all the corruption and all. You've got to pay into the system and then the system stops the poaching. I paid seven hundred dollars to shoot an aardvark. Do you know aardvarks? It's sort of like an anteater. You don't want to confuse it with an aardwolf. An aardwolf costs less as there are more of them.'

'And how,' said Claudia Bellingham, 'does the money help to conserve the animals that you shoot?'

'You pay it to the chiefs, to the authorities. They keep out the poachers. I'd like to shoot 'em all.'

'Poachers?' said Randy Sidewinder.

'Sure, I'd shoot them all.'

I sensed on my left that Claire could not control herself any longer. 'And how much do you suppose they would charge per poacher?' she asked.

'Hell, I don't know,' said Hiram Sidewinder, 'not much, I expect.' He gave a snort of laughter. 'There's not much you can do with them. You can't eat 'em. You can't put their heads on the wall.'

At the end of the table Edouard had risen to address the Bellinghams. 'I expect you ladies would like a little time in your hut before Moses collects you at nine o'clock. You need take nothing with you apart from cameras and binoculars. He will carry your packed lunches in his rucksack. Also, you need not worry about sunscreen or hats. The jungle canopy is very effective.'

As the Bellinghams departed towards their hut, Hiram Sidewinder turned towards Claire and myself. 'Hell,' he said, 'I hope we didn't say anything to offend the ladies.'

'I think they entered into the general spirit of things,' I said. 'More coffee?'

On the way back to our hut, Claire and I passed Edouard, who had escorted the Bellingham sisters and Moses to the start of their day's safari. He stopped and rolled his eyes to the back of his head. 'My God,' he said, 'three more days of this.'

'Oh, I don't know,' I said, 'it wasn't too bad. Quite interesting. I suspect that was the first time the Bellingham sisters have ever felt like killing anything.'

'They weren't the only ones,' said Edouard. 'Anyway they appeared happy enough. Moses will give them a good day. But

I'm worried. There is still no sign of the chimps. There are the noises that we have all heard but no sign of the Serole troupe. They have now been gone for two weeks.'

Claire laid a hand on his forearm. 'It will be all right. If anyone can find them, Moses will.'

'But that's the thing. I have never known him so apprehensive. He seemed almost unwilling to leave. He is not unwell. It is unlike him.' Edouard turned and surveyed the silent jungle. Then he looked up to the mountains beyond, on the top of which cloud could be seen accumulating. The sun still shone but the wind over the lake had noticeably increased. The waves were beginning to mount and, at the landing stage, the covered boat pitched and swayed.

'Storm coming?' I said.

He nodded. 'Could be quite fierce. I will secure that boat.' He left and Claire and I walked back to our veranda. Unusually and instinctively we held hands. We spent the day together, avoiding the Sidewinders and revisiting the kitchens and staff areas set back in the jungle, fifty metres from the lodge. There were two new members of staff but apart from that we knew them all well from the years we had spent there, blissfully happy, absorbed in each other and in the joys of primate research. From the kitchen we took bread, cheese, tomatoes and salami and, from the store room, a bottle of South African wine. It was a ritual we had performed a hundred times before and, as we carried them back to our hut, the sense of unease departed. We enjoyed a good lunch and spent the afternoon in bed.

We had both fallen asleep and were awoken simultaneously by the noise which had begun in the jungle behind us. We lay silent, looking at each other, alert with concentration. It was the same noise. It resembled the hunting call of male chimpanzees but delivered in chorus. Orchestrated. This I had never heard. Chimpanzees employ calls as signals between members of a hunting group. As such they are ragged, sometimes discordant. Individual shrieks will sometimes blend or, more often, react to each other. They are signals of pursuit, high in the canopies of the forest, organising the strategy of entrapment and kill. These were different. The calls and shrieks amounted to something approaching harmony, a definite, sustained paean of triumph. They were repeated along the mountainside from deep in the forest and closer to the margin of the lake. Then they died away.

'Christ,' I said, 'have you ever heard that before?'

Claire was shaking her head. 'Never, not before last night. I simply would not recognise it.'

I looked at my watch and then out to the veranda. Beyond it the sky was now overcast. The wind came in gusts and the movement of the forest and the thatch dominated the increasing sounds of the waves.

'The Bellinghams will be back,' I said, 'and Moses. They will be having tea. Let us go and join them.'

But they were not. As we approached the lodge we found Edouard standing at the door of the bar. He held a radio in one hand and was scanning the beach and the jungle beyond. When we approached he motioned us to one side and elevated the binoculars which hung around his neck. Slowly he moved them across the canopy of the trees, then he left them fall, took up the hand radio and activated the call button which glowed red on the tiny dial. He spoke urgently into the mike. 'Moses, come in, will you, please.' He released the button and looked at the screen. It remained blank and silent.

He looked at me and shrugged. 'Nothing, nothing. The last contact was at one thirty. They were approximately four kilometres into the forest. Up there,' he said, indicating the first ridge in the jungle as it rose above the beach. 'They hadn't found any chimps and had stopped to eat. Moses sounded worried. He said that they were coming straight back and then I think I heard something on his radio. It was like these strange calls, but softer, as though it was close behind him. I distinctly heard a human cry. One of the Bellingham sisters, I think. Then there was silence. That was it, nothing else. I tried again at two thirty. The radio seemed to be open and I heard soft chimp noises. Then silence again.'

He lifted the binoculars and gazed at the top of the trees. I knew that he was looking for the movement of chimpanzees but there was none. He dropped the binoculars again and stated the obvious. 'If they had set out at that time they would have been here by half past two, three at the latest. Moses knows better than anyone that all tours must be out of the forest by four thirty. It is now,' he said, consulting his watch, 'half past five.'

As he looked at his watch I saw the first splashes of rain on its surface. Thunder rumbled in the mountains and after a brief interval, a flash of sheet lightning announced the beginnings of the storm. It drove us inside and into the corner of the bar. Further into the lodge the Sidewinders occupied the sitting area. Beyond them Jolyon Downside and Cindy Applebloom were talking to John Boxe, teacups in their hands. Edouard crossed behind the bar, picked up a whisky glass and said, 'Drink?' It was an invitation to a conspiracy. I glanced at Claire and we both nodded. He poured three generous glasses of whisky, splashed water into all of them and passed two across the bar. When he took his first pull of the liquor I could see that his hand was shaking. He set down his glass and looked straight at me.

'I think you were right. I should not have let this happen. Something may be very, very wrong and Moses knew it.'

I held his gaze. 'What are you going to do?'

'I don't know. I don't even know what it is but I can sense a danger and then there are these damn noises. I have never heard them before and neither have you.'

I said, 'We have got to evacuate the guests.'

Edouard nodded. 'I suppose that is right. But it cannot be done tonight. The storm is coming. The boat cannot be moved. Tomorrow is possible, but probably the day after.'

Claire said, 'The helicopter?'

Edouard nodded. 'I have already radioed a request to Base. Reception is very bad. There is an electric storm right along the lake shore. Even if they received my request, no helicopter would fly in this. The important thing is not to cause a panic. Moses may yet return. In the meantime we should rearrange the accommodation. We cannot have anyone sleeping at the far end of the beach. You two and Jolyon and Cindy can move into the lodge. The Sidewinders have the biggest and closest hut. They should all stay in there. Bo Fang can go to the old researchers' hut by the kitchens. I have issued firearms to Benedict and Boniface with instructions that they should keep them out of sight. Is there anything else I can do?'

Claire and I shook our heads. Edouard said, 'Right, I will organise a meeting in the library at six thirty. I should be grateful if you would come too.' We all three drained our glasses, nodded briefly to each other and made our way along the length of the lodge towards our fellow guests, who were in the process of finishing their tea and biscuits.

CHAPTER 6

The meeting began at six thirty. It was held in the library area on the first floor of the mess building. This room was open on two sides, one providing a view across the darkening lake, the other showing the foothills of the forested mountains. They appeared closer in the gathering gloom. Present at the meeting were myself, Claire and Edouard. Hiram Sidewinder III sprawled across a sofa next to his wife, Winnie. The twins, Josh and Randy, considered old enough to attend, sat behind their parents on two chairs. On another sofa, Jolyon Downside assumed an elegant actor's pose close to Cindy Applebloom, on whose thigh he rested a gentle and contracting hand. Violet Sidewinder, aged twelve, was told that she was too young for the business at hand and, with some reluctance, her parents had allowed her to remain in the mess area, where she could be heard faintly, talking to a member of the catering staff. The tracker guides, Benedict and Boniface, sat behind Edouard and me.

A brisk and increasing wind rustled the thatch above our heads. On the lake the boat fretted and groaned at its mooring, tight-lashed against the impending storm. Over the mountains just visible above the forest occasional flashes of lightning could be seen, followed by the sound of thunder rolling in the far distance. The generator, fired up to replace the solar batteries, chuntered gently and evenly from the direction of the staff quarters. Absent from the meeting were the Bellingham sisters, Pat and Claudia, and the senior tracker guide, Moses. The Sidewinders noisily discussed a domestic issue whilst Jolyon Downside and Cindy Applebloom whispered in quiet and close communion.

At twenty to seven the last member of the gathering, Yojo Bo Fang, the Chinese research student, climbed the wooden stairs, deposited three library books on the low table, looked around for a seat and finally selected a stool with a padded zebra-skin cover. Edouard cleared his throat, silence fell and he began. His faultless English was delivered with his cultivated French accent. It was calculated to instil a Gallic calm in his audience, all of whom, I noticed, had visited the bar and who now held various glasses of assorted liquor. I had a glass of beer. Hiram Sidewinder held a tumbler of whisky, dark and barely diluted. He took a long sip as Edouard began.

'Thank you for coming to this meeting, which concerns a matter of some seriousness. I suspect that some of you are already aware of the main reason for our gathering. As you know, Pat and Claudia Bellingham went on an early safari into the forest, trying to find the Serole troupe, which we believed was approximately five kilometres up the mountain. They had packed lunches and bottles of water. I am afraid that they have not returned. There is a house rule that all excursions into the forest must reach a conclusion by four thirty. That is,' he said, unnecessarily consulting his watch, 'over two hours ago. We are obviously concerned.'

Hiram Sidewinder intervened. 'Have you had any contact? Have they got a radio with them?'

'They have, of course, a radio operated on our local transmitter. The last contact was at half past one. Since then they have not attempted to call me. I have been repeatedly calling since two o'clock. I am afraid that this has been largely unsuccessful.'

'Largely? What do you mean, largely?' Sidewinder leaned forward and gestured with his whisky glass. 'What does that mean, largely? Either you have had communication or you haven't.'

'At about half past two, when I called, Moses's radio appeared to be open.'

'What does that mean? Appeared?'

'Please, Mr Sidewinder, I will tell you all that I know. The radio channel appeared to be open but there was no human response.'

'*Human*? What did you hear, God?'

'No, Mr Sidewinder, it was not God. It was the noise of animals.'

'What animals? What do you mean, chimpanzees?'

'Possibly.' Edouard held up his hand against any further interruption. 'Possibly. I say possibly because the reception was very poor and the noise, while it resembled the hunting call of a male chimpanzee, was not one that I have ever heard before – and I have over twenty years' experience with chimpanzees in general and with this troupe in particular. Apart from that brief contact the radio has remained dead.'

In the pause that followed this information the soft patrician tones of Jolyon Downside filled the room. He spoke generally but stared fixedly at Cindy Applebloom barely two feet away.

'Is it possible,' he said, 'that there has been some kind of accident? A ravine, a crevasse, an overhanging creeper? These are, after all, ladies of a certain age. The jungle conceals many dangers. Is it not possible . . .'

Edouard nodded his head. 'That is of course a possibility. I do not want to cause you any alarm. Moses is my most experienced guide and tracker. He is in his forties and has spent his entire life in these mountains. He carries with him emergency medical supplies and fresh water in addition to the radio. Accidents can, of course, always happen and cannot be ruled out. Tomorrow we will send out a search party. It is far too dangerous to walk in the jungle at night. We have excellent trackers here who will find where they have gone.' Edouard paused, surveyed his audience and then continued. 'At present we have no knowledge but can only speculate or guess. Nonetheless I think it would be wise if we took a number of sensible precautions.'

'Precautions!' The repetition snapped from Hiram Sidewinder like a gunshot. 'Precautions? What kind of precautions can we take?'

'Changes in our accommodation are necessary. Mr Downside and Miss Applebloom, you have the furthest hut; I suggest you move, if you would, to number 1 just over there, which is empty. Mr Bo Fang may move to the old researchers' quarters, next to the staff quarters and kitchen. Mr Sidewinder, you have the main guest house, which has three separate bedrooms. I suggest that we move your children in with you for the time being.'

Sidewinder thrust out both arms and seemed about to rise. 'Now wait a minute, just wait a minute, we are circling the wagons, right? That's what we are doing. We're circling the wagons, but against what? Where are the Indians? What are the Indians? What are we taking precautions against?'

Mrs Sidewinder interrupted her husband, her voice raising a full octave all of a sudden in dreadful revelation.

'*Muslims*,' she cried. 'Muslims, Jee Hardists. That's it, it's

44

Muslim Jee Hardists. They have kidnapped the Bellinghams. Oh my God.'

She rose to her feet and clasped both hands to her bosom. Immediately behind her, Josh and Randy Sidewinder rose in unison to their mother's support. Edouard held up both arms.

'Please, please, Mrs Sidewinder, what you suggest is totally impossible. There are no Islamic jihadists in Tanzania. If there were they would have to travel through fifty kilometres of uncharted jungle to reach us. Either that or they would have to come by boat across Lake Tanganyika and there are *no such boats.* And even if such dysfunctional terrorists existed they would have no interest in the Bellingham sisters. English sisters of limited means do not attract fundamentalists.'

'What if they didn't want the Bellingham sisters? What if they were after my husband? He is a *dentist* from Memphis. He's got the biggest practice in Tennessee. He's insured for twenty million dollars and he's a Baptist lay preacher. Oh my God.'

Edouard tried again. 'Mrs Sidewinder, will you please calm down. I have lived in Tanzania for thirty years. I know the local people, their habits and their customs. There are some Muslims in Zanzibar, but that is hundreds of kilometres away and they are not jihadists. They are good Muslims.'

Mrs Sidewinder thrust her sons aside and fixed Edouard with a look of utter contempt.

'*Good* Muslims,' she hissed. After a dramatic pause she threw her head backwards and uttered a single word. '*Ha!*' She collapsed back on to her seat. Immediately beside her Hiram Sidewinder took a large draught of whisky and narrowed his eyes. He ignored Edouard and looked directly at me. When he spoke his voice was quiet and even.

'I think,' he said, 'that there is something we are not being told. I think there is something you know that we do not know. I am right, aren't I?'

I am a poor liar but also I sensed immediately discovery. Without looking at Edouard I returned Sidewinder's stare and gave the briefest nod.

'Right,' he said. 'Let's have it out now. What's the secret?'

To my left I was aware of Jolyon Downside and Cindy Applebloom leaning forward into the silence.

'I do not believe,' I said, 'that human beings are responsible for the disappearance of Pat and Claudia Bellingham.' I paused, took a deep breath and continued. 'I believe it may be animals.'

Beside me Edouard stiffened. He radiated disapproval as Sidewinder said, 'Animals, animals? What animals? Leopard? Hyena? What the hell have you got up here?'

'No, not leopard or hyena. I think it may be chimpanzees.'

Mrs Sidewinder got ahead of her husband. 'Chimpanzees? But we read your literature. It says, quite clearly, chimpanzees have never been known to cause significant injury to people. I remember it quite clearly. "They may be a little boisterous and pushy but they are never violent."'

I looked at Edouard, who stared back. I turned to the Sidewinders. 'If I am right, and it is very possible that I am not right, then this is not a normal chimpanzee.'

'Not *normal*?' Hiram Sidewinder held my eyes, his own narrowed to slits. 'Not normal? How is it not normal?'

'I believe he is aberrant.'

'What do you mean, aberrant?'

'Well, to start with, I believe he killed his own kind.'

There was a period of silence before Sidewinder said, 'Who is this ape anyway? What's he called? How old is he? We've got a right to know, for Christ's sake.'

'He must be twenty years of age. His name is Ronald.'

'*Ronald*? What kind of name is that for a chimp? Why is he called Ronald?'

'He's called Ronald after Ronald Reagan. It was a time when we were calling all the chimps after American politicians. One was called Nixon, others Kennedy, Truman and Carter. Ronald's mother was already called Regan. Look, I will tell you it all. He was an aberration. He was driven out ten years ago by his own troupe. He was a delinquent.'

'Christ. That was ten years ago and now you think he's come back?'

'Yes.'

'What makes you think he came back?'

'He killed another male.'

'But that's what happens. That's what chimpanzees do. That's what animals do. They kill the weak.'

'He dismembered the body.'

'He what? He dismembered the body?'

'Yes, only . . .'

'Only what?'

'He couldn't have done it alone.'

'You mean he's got a gang? A gang of mad apes?'

'More than one, perhaps several.'

'But that's normal, that's how they deal with the hierarchy. Caesar and Brutus and all that.'

47

'If there is more than one, they do not come from the Serole troupe. We know that. We know our chimpanzees. There are none in the troupe that would follow him and certainly none that would kill in this way.'

Mrs Sidewinder's Southern accent had become thick with the gin. 'Wet liberals, you mean. That's what they are, wet liberals hanging around with human beings.'

Before I could reply, Jolyon Downside spoke quietly. 'I wonder if I may just ask a question? If he was driven out of the troupe ten years ago and disappeared, how do you know that he is responsible for this . . . murder? Apart from the grisly details, is there any other means of identification?'

I looked at Edouard, who nodded with resignation. 'Yes,' I said, 'there is. He has his own signature. When he was growing up in the troupe he was delinquent, out of control. He appeared particularly to loathe humans, researchers, academics, tourists, the whole lot. He had his own sign of contempt.'

'And what was that?'

'He would turn his rear end towards you and defecate. That's how he got his name.'

'Hell,' said Hiram Sidewinder, who had just drained his whisky. 'That's not aberrant behaviour. All animals shit in public. They don't give a damn. When you have killed as many animals as I have you know about animal behaviour. You know they don't give a damn. They just shit all over the place.'

'Not as a deliberate part of a public display. And . . .' I paused, anticipating the reaction that my next words would inevitably have. 'And when he had finished whatever the act of thievery, sexual violence or bullying was, he would deliberately defecate and stand over it and grin.'

The entire Sidewinder family exploded with derision. 'He'd grin? Apes don't grin. They bare their teeth as a warning or a submission. Christ, apes don't grin!'

I stared back at him, aware of the weakness of my case. 'This one did. He did not bare his teeth, he curled his lip. It was . . . unmistakable. And,' I continued as best I could, 'he would half close an eye. It was as close to a wink as I have seen.' I was conscious of the silence that had fallen in the room when I added: 'It was quite horrible.'

Sidewinder looked at his empty glass. 'Christ, I need another drink, but tell me this. Did anybody else see this? Did anyone else know about this shitting or winking or was it just you?'

'It was well known. Many of the trackers and staff saw it. It accounted for his nickname.'

'Oh yeah? And what was his name?'

'Dump, because that's what he used to do. Dump.'

Sidewinder rose and crossed to the stairs. 'I am going to get myself a drink and when I come back we're going to decide what to do. But just let us get this straight. You think he is back, this psychotic ape, that he's out there, *Ronald Dump*. You think he's back and you think he's got something to do with the Bellinghams disappearing. I'll be back but I need a drink.'

The whole party followed him. As they descended the stairs Edouard stood before me. 'I thought,' he said softly, 'we were going to avoid panic.'

'It is the truth. It would be far worse if they believed the forest was full of Islamic extremists. If the Bellinghams do not return the truth is bound to emerge. If they do return, then no harm is done.'

'No harm! No harm! It is the end of the lodge, my home. If this becomes public, if the idea of Dump spreads, we will *never* open again. No harm!' He turned and followed his guests into the bar.

CHAPTER 7

When the guests reassembled twenty minutes later they were led by Hiram Sidewinder and his wife. All were present with the exception of Yojo Bo Fang and Violet Sidewinder. Everyone had replenished their drinks and Sidewinder carried a tumbler half full of whisky which appeared to be neat. His wife had a glass containing clear liquid, ice and lemon. The slight grimace that she made on first sampling her liquor indicated that the gin was very strong. Everyone resumed their seats and, by apparent prior arrangement, deferred to the Sidewinders.

'My wife,' said Hiram Sidewinder, 'has given the matter some thought. She has reached a conclusion which I think may fit the facts.' He nodded towards his wife, who spoke with an earnest Southern drawl markedly increased by the consumption of gin.

'We do not think,' she began, 'that this unhappy disappearance of three people today is the work of animals. Even a sudden attack by the most ferocious animals would be unlikely to disrupt urgent emergency radio communication. Furthermore, I have been rereading the material that we received about this lodge and the chimpanzees here. You say, quite clearly, that the chimpanzees have never been known seriously to injure human beings. The Serole group habituated around the lodge have been there for fifty years. The other seven hundred chimpanzees are scattered in families across the mountains and the forest and avoid human contact at all costs. So I am driven to return to the conclusion that I have already voiced.' She paused and held up her gin by way of added emphasis. Her voice rose an octave. '*Muslims.*' Seeing the disbelief on my face she made a dismissive gesture with her glass. 'Not just ordinary terrorist Muslims. *Jee Hardist, conservationist Muslims.*'

Before I could reply Hiram Sidewinder joined in. 'You see, maybe you don't know but I have been shooting in the Selous hunting park. I have been shooting there for three weeks. Now in the course of that enterprise I unhappily shot a giraffe. I say straight away that I did not intend to shoot the giraffe. I was aiming to shoot a leopard that was in a tree but the giraffe wandered across my line of sight and, unhappily, I shot the giraffe. Even more unhappily, my guides insisted on taking a photograph of myself with my foot on the giraffe and within days it had gone viral. The photograph, that is. It was plastered literally over the whole of the world's press. Very unpleasant things were said about the size of a giraffe and the level of marksmanship that would be necessary to kill such an animal. Some of the articles and comments were very wounding indeed. It was revealed that I was a dentist from Memphis and that my practice was the biggest practice in Tennessee. Several newspapers commented in a snide and unpleasant way on the number of teeth that a giraffe has. I don't give a goddamn how many teeth a giraffe has. I do not practise orthodontics on giraffes or any other animal. As a result of the publicity my practice in Memphis has been under siege and I have received the most obscene threats and communications. I thought that we would be safe if we remained in Africa but I reckoned without your Muslim problem. *Jee Hard*. It is our view that these unfortunate people have been kidnapped by Islamic conservationist *Jee Hardists* and that the real target was myself.'

This speech was accompanied by vigorous nodding from Winnie Sidewinder and her two sons. Beyond them Jolyon Downside and Cindy Applebloom appeared less convinced, while the trackers Benedict and Boniface stared fixedly at the ceiling. I glanced at Edouard, who nodded at me to reply.

'Mrs Sidewinder,' I said, pitching my voice between patience and condescension, 'I do appreciate your fears and your concerns and I am grateful for your theory, but I am afraid, for various reasons, it is completely untenable.' I raised my left hand and carefully counted off arguments on the extended fingers. 'First, as I have told you, although there are Muslims in Tanzania the vast majority are located in Zanzibar, which is hundreds of kilometres away. There are Muslims in the Democratic Republic of Congo and also in Rwanda, but they are on the far side of Lake Tanganyika and have no known connections with jihad or fundamentalism. Secondly, the followers of jihad have no conservationist interests. On the contrary, their main fundamentalist group, Al-Shabab, funds its activities by poaching elephant, lion and rhino and they would be wholly unmoved by the death of a giraffe. Thirdly, even the most fanatical and purblind Muslim terrorist would be unlikely to mistake the Bellingham sisters for an American dentist. I think we can certainly discount terrorist activity. But above all, let us not concentrate on such a theory and thereby overlook what is a far more dangerous possibility.'

This, I noticed, had the desired effect. Expressions of disbelief which had previously emanated from the Sidewinder family were replaced by urgent concern. Jolyon Downside and Cindy Applebloom moved closer together. I continued.

'You are right about the behaviour and history of the chimpanzees, certainly the communities that surround this lodge. In forty years no serious harm has ever been known to occur to human beings. We are regarded, if you like, as welcome immigrants. Occasionally they steal food but otherwise they regard us with nothing more than curiosity. As to the hundreds of chimpanzees that live in the mountains, it is true that they rarely come into contact with humans at all. Occasionally the younger ones give sounds and signals of alarm but otherwise there is peaceful co-existence. But I repeat the concerns that I aired before. There is undoubtedly a delinquent chimpanzee at large. He is an aberration, possibly together with one or two others.'

Hiram Sidewinder intervened. 'Ronald Dump.'

'Precisely. For reasons which I will not go into I believed, when I left Serole ten years ago, that he was dead. Now I believe him to be alive. He has undoubtedly been complicit in the violent death and dismembering of a male in the Serole troupe. I am told that there have been similar occurrences in the past two weeks.' I paused while the information was digested and comments exchanged between the members of my audience. 'So we must assume this is Dump and also that he is not acting alone.'

'A gang!' said Hiram Sidewinder.

'Perhaps, but that, in itself, gives rise to serious conclusions. It is unknown for male chimpanzees to assume that role in a troupe other than their own. If they try they are immediately ousted and, if necessary, killed. One of the reasons why we presumed Dump to be dead was the fact that he had left the troupe and did not return. Male chimpanzees in such circumstances, however powerful and delinquent, never survive. Then there are two other things to consider. The Serole troupe have effectively disappeared. They have not been seen for two weeks. Worse, they have not been heard. A troupe can be heard over a wide area, sometimes as much as five kilometres. Here there is silence.'

Hiram Sidewinder intervened. 'What are the noises that we heard last night? What of them? What were they?'

'Whatever they were, they certainly did not come from the Serole troupe or any other family of chimpanzees. I have never heard calls like that before. They resembled the hunting calls of chimpanzees, normally associated with the pursuit of monkeys, but these calls were static and came from many directions and locations. Furthermore, they appeared to be in chorus or co-ordinated.'

'Holy shit,' said Hiram Sidewinder, 'holy shit. Are you saying that this psychopathic ape has organised a kind of *rebellion*?'

'I think rebellion would be the wrong word. We do not rule over the chimpanzees, we study them.'

'That may not be what they think.'

'We should never intervene or interfere in their affairs, however difficult or violent they may be. We allow nature to take its course. What I am saying is that we do not know. It could be nothing, a new phenomenon, but it would be wise to take the precautions that have already been outlined.'

Jolyon Downside raised his hand, a mock childhood request for attention. 'May I ask,' he said, 'when the management of this lodge became aware of this state of affairs?'

I deferred to Edouard, who shifted uncomfortably in his seat. 'The deaths that have been mentioned, the details of those were known last week.'

'Last week!' said Jolyon Downside, glancing at Cindy Applebloom. 'Last week! And we were not informed? You took no steps to cancel the bookings?'

'I am afraid not. We could not assess the seriousness of the position and besides . . .'

'Besides?'

'Besides, as Arthur has said, in our many years of experience there has never been any danger in this lodge. I would like to emphasise that there has never been any danger.'

Hiram Sidewinder finished his whisky and assumed the tone of a professional. 'I think the time has come for some action. You may know a lot about chimpanzees but I know a lot about animal behaviour. When you have killed as many animals as I have you know something about their behaviour and I know this. When an animal goes bad, and I mean bad, when he becomes a killer, there is only one thing to do and that is to shoot him, find him and shoot him. Whatever has happened to the Bellinghams, that, at least, is what we should do to this Dump. Find him and finish him, and I am ready to undertake precisely that task.'

Murmurs of approval came from the rest of the Sidewinder family.

'Now what firearms do you have in the lodge?'

'We only have two firearms, both AK-47s issued by the Tanzanian National Parks Authority.'

'AK-47s,' said Hiram Sidewinder in a tone of total contempt. 'AK-47s are peashooters. You need 404s or 407s, real guns. I have got five such firearms in my box which you have in your office, so I suggest you open that box and hand the guns to my sons and myself so that we may pursue this Dump immediately.'

Edouard rose from his chair. 'Mr Sidewinder, there has not been hunting in these mountains for sixty years, not in living memory. To allow it, in any way, would destroy the relationship we have built up with the chimpanzees. Also, as you know, Tanzanian law provides me with the authority to hold these guns in secure circumstances while you are a guest at the lodge. It specifically forbids me to allow their use or, indeed, to allow them to be taken from the secure box.'

Hiram Sidewinder was also standing. 'But these are my guns, my weapons, and this ape has got to be shot. Don't you see? It is the divine will that I am here in order to carry out this task.'

Behind him Jolyon Downside spoke in a voice calculated to calm. 'Would it not be a better plan for us all quietly to leave the lodge at the first available moment? Doubtless some form of refund can be arranged in these circumstances. Tonight we must obviously take precautions but tomorrow we should leave and hand this problem over to the authorities.'

Edouard gave a brief nod. 'That is undoubtedly true,' he said. 'Unhappily there can be no question of leaving tomorrow. The storm over the lake has already begun. There is clearly foul weather in the mountains. We could not risk the boat and helicopters will not fly except in . . .'

He did not finish his sentence. A loud human scream came from the beach, so loud it echoed against the mountains.

'My God,' shouted Winnie Sidewinder. 'Violet!'

CHAPTER 8

Extracts from Serole Research Log, Day 15

23 May 2002

Observed the extraordinary behaviour of the young chimpanzee known as Ronald. He is apparently eight years old but he is very large for his age. His name comes from the new practice of identification. Having exhausted the classics the lodge resorted to American presidents, starting with Lincoln. Ronald's mother was already Regan (from King Lear*) so her next infant was given President Reagan's Christian name. He stills rides on his mother's back, which is unusual and slightly shocking considering his size. Infant chimpanzees normally ride in a prone position, their heads pressed against the mother's fur, hands gripping both sides of her body. Normally, like humans, they will walk independently at one and a half or two years old and certainly before eight. Regan is a senior female and should, by now, have further offspring. It appears that Ronald remains her only child. What is strange is that he rides on her back bolt upright. With one hand he grips the back of his mother's neck, his two legs hanging to either side. Periodically he kicks hard with his heels. Occasionally Regan reacts but not as a mother. She gives instead the submissive call of surrender.*

Moses says he has seen it before. He said, 'He bully his mother very bad. He not only kick her but he bite her face and her genitals. He is a very big chimpanzee for his age. It is very unusual behaviour.' I asked whether Regan had given birth to any other babies after Ronald. He said that Regan had become pregnant twice in the last two years. In accordance with normal practice she had disappeared into the bush when her time came to give birth.

'We have never seen any babies,' said Moses. 'Either they die or they have been done in.'

10 April 2004

Two years at Serole. The happiest four years of my life. I have become a part of the Serole family. You can become too close to them. In the black, unblinking eyes of a chimpanzee you begin to discern all manner of subtleties beyond the crude distinctions of personality, strength and weakness. Ajax is a case in point. He is now the alpha male. It is a role which requires displays of testosterone and occasional violence, anger and impatience. But he enjoys obvious support, particularly from the females. Gertrude is his principal companion. For long periods they sit together, 'grooming and communing' as Edouard says. This is accompanied by indecipherable murmurs and grunts. It is a gentle, persuasive language that no one, not even Goodall or Fossey, has translated. Impossible not to apply the construction of human power. She is his consigliere. *The complex relations and hierarchies of the troupe, sixty apes strong, are reported, perhaps discussed, judged. While she communicates he has a habit of stroking his chin. Chimpanzees do not possess beards but the gesture has a mandarin, Confucian quality nonetheless.*

I am allowed to be a witness. I sit close by with my notebook, tolerated and ignored. He also enjoys the hegemony of the larger subordinate males, particularly Hector, Horatio and Brutus. They are younger. One day one of them will succeed him. For the present he keeps them close and they form the nucleus of a hunting group, pursuing red-tailed and colobus monkeys with deadly organised precision through the high canopy of the forest.

25 June 2004

A new research graduate has arrived, Claire Watkins from Warwick. She is tall and very beautiful. She appears to tolerate me. I am thinking less about the chimpanzees.

14 February 2005

I am concerned about the relationship between Regan and Ronald, her son. He is now eleven years of age but nearly fully grown, enormous and powerful. He is a bully and his mother is his primary target. As a result of her son's attacks, bite marks are often visible on her face and body and nails have been torn from her fingers. She has become very thin. She is unable to climb or to navigate the trees in search of food. Edouard insists on a non-intervention policy. Whatever occurs between the chimpanzees is to be recorded and studied as a phenomenon. Interference of any kind is anathema. I have repeatedly told him that Regan will die or be killed without help or at least the provision of food. He shrugs and says it is all very sad for humans but for the apes it is nature's course. We have argued about that. 'My dear Arthur,' he says, 'this is not a zoo. We have no more responsibility to protect them from themselves than we do to protect them from famine. Ronald was born seven years before you arrived at Serole. He has abused his mother sexually and physically since he was able to walk. But it is a matter of academic interest. That is all.'

26 February 2005
This afternoon I helped unload the boat at the jetty. It included the
week's provisions. Once they were in the kitchen I selected a box of
assorted fruit for myself and made my way to my tent through the
fringes of the jungle. I had reached the clearing behind the lodge
when I saw Regan. She was crouched against a tall mahogany,
practically invisible in the surrounding bush. She saw me but did
not move. I could see that she was shivering with a mixture of
fear and malnutrition. I made up my mind immediately. Edouard
was wrong. I walked to a position within five metres of the
chimpanzee, upended my box on the ground, retreated to the edge
of the clearing and removed my notebook from my pocket.

I waited five minutes before she left the shadow of the tree. She
descended on the food and began to devour it, quickly, without
selection. She did not hear Ronald arrive behind her until he
snatched the fruit from her hand and with the same movement
clubbed her across the face. Instantly she began the gibbering
sound of submissive distress and retreated to crouch at the edge
of the forest. Ronald picked up my box and examined it, his face
disappearing inside. He then looked around the clearing and saw
me. For a moment he stared, then he reared up on his legs and
hurled the box at my head. His aim was poor but he looked at
me from his full height. His upper lip curled back, showing his
teeth, before he slowly turned, deliberately squatted and vented
himself in an unmistakable gesture of contempt. He turned to his
mother and slowly began to advance towards her. At that moment
I became aware of movement in the trees behind me. I watched
as first Ajax, then Brutus and Horatio moved across the open
ground. Gertrude joined them. Within seconds the three male
chimpanzees were in direct confrontation with Ronald. Horatio

and Brutus moved to either side, closing him in. For a minute he returned their stares, then dropped to all fours and began the familiar kuk, kuk, kuk, *the sound of submission. Ajax half turned away, then delivered a massive blow to the side of Ronald's head. More followed. The beating was systematic and without remorse. It lasted a matter of minutes and involved Ajax rising repeatedly to full height the better to judge the point of impact. Finally it stopped. Ronald continued to make weak noises from the floor. Ajax and his companions departed without acknowledging my presence. Gertrude and Regan followed. When they passed both looked straight at me without expression or sound as they disappeared into the forest.*

CHAPTER 9

Randy and Josh Sidewinder were first down the stairs, leaping the wide treads two by two. When they reached the bottom Josh turned just in time to catch his mother, who had fallen on the last flight. Hiram Sidewinder clasped his wife before the family began running along the beach. Violet Sidewinder's hut could be seen sixty metres distant. On its veranda a hurricane lamp guttered in the wind now blowing in gusts from the storm across the lake. All four of them carried the torches that were provided by the lodge, their beams illuminating the rain now falling incessantly from the moonless sky. Behind them Claire and I and Jolyon Downside made a slower pace, followed by Cindy Applebloom. Next came Edouard. Last came John Boxe, the photographer, who, it subsequently transpired, was recording the events on his Leica camera in both still and movie mode. Twenty metres ahead of us I saw Randy and Josh Sidewinder leap on to the veranda and disappear into the hut. By the time we arrived the front curtains had been thrown back, revealing the immediate interior to be empty. A small number of clothes lay untidily across the bed but otherwise the room appeared undisturbed. A mosquito net, lowered by the staff, fluttered in the wind. From the far interior of the hut, Winnie Sidewinder could be heard helplessly shouting the name of her daughter. 'Violet! Violet!'

Hiram Sidewinder emerged back into the room. 'She's not here,' he said, staring at Edouard. 'She's not here so where the hell is she?'

Edouard's reply was cut short by the noise which began in the forest and rose steadily, repeated from site after site, extending into the mountains beyond. It was the same sound. A strange mutant noise. The scream of the hunting chimpanzee but repeated in triumphal chorus along the line of the shore.

'My God,' said Hiram Sidewinder, 'my God. Can you hear that?'

As the cries faded into the night they were replaced by a human voice calling from the direction of the lodge.

'Ma, Mama, where are you?'

'Violet,' cried Winnie Sidewinder and disappeared into the night.

In approximately the same order and at the same speed the entire party returned across the beach to the lodge. By the time we arrived Winnie Sidewinder had her daughter clutched to her bosom and was offering her benedictions. 'Thank God, thank God. My darling, my darling, you are safe.'

Violet Sidewinder gently removed herself from her mother. 'Yeah, I am safe, of course I'm safe. I've been in the kitchen with Erasmus. What happened to you? What's the matter with him?' She pointed to Jolyon Downside, who was leaning heavily against the wall of the lodge, apparently unused to running on soft sand.

'Never mind, never mind, darling,' said Hiram Sidewinder, 'you're safe, but why did you scream?'

'Scream?' said Violet Sidewinder, revealing a bottle of Coca-Cola in her right hand. 'Scream? I didn't scream. I've been drinking Coke.'

Silence fell, which accompanied a universal calculation of numbers and identities.

Edouard stated the conclusion. 'Where is Yojo Bo Fang?'

'Who?' said Hiram Sidewinder.

'The Chinese guy,' said Randy Sidewinder. 'The one in the glasses. He never says anything.'

'Maybe he's okay,' said Josh Sidewinder.

'But that scream,' said Cindy Applebloom, 'was terrible. I used to be a nurse and I know a scream of terror and pain.'

'We should go and look at his hut,' said Hiram Sidewinder. 'Where is it?'

'It's further along the beach,' said Edouard, pointing a finger back in the direction of the huts. 'The last one you can see from here. I'll go.'

'Hell, no,' said Hiram Sidewinder, 'you can't go on your own and unarmed. Whatever we do we should all stick together. Get your guides out here with those guns.'

Edouard looked at me and I nodded. 'He's right. It may be nothing but we need Benedict and Boniface with us and I agree about the guns.'

Edouard nodded and resumed a semblance of control. 'Everybody, please wait here. Within the lodge you are all warm and safe. I will get our guides.' He disappeared into the night in the direction of the staff quarters. The Sidewinders gathered together and uttered sounds of relief and condolence. Jolyon Downside and Cindy Applebloom whispered by the bar. Unknown and unnoticed, John Boxe continued to take photographs, and I spoke quietly to Claire.

'What do you think?'

She looked straight back into my eyes. 'I think this is

beginning to be very dangerous. Nothing remotely like this has ever happened before. If I am honest I am a little frightened.'

Edouard returned with Benedict and Boniface, both carrying the AK-47 rifles issued to accredited guides by the Tanzanian National Parks Authority. A measure of calm confidence began to return.

'Well, I suggest we travel in a line, two by two,' said Edouard in his manager's role. 'There are umbrellas over there. Let us stick together and go visit Mr Bo Fang.'

Six umbrellas were selected from the stand, torches were illuminated and we made our way across the beach. Passing Violet Sidewinder's hut, we proceeded towards the hut of Yojo Bo Fang, the front of which was lit by a hurricane lamp and, increasingly, by the beams of eight torches.

When we reached the hut we all instinctively crowded on to the veranda, out of the driving rain. Before us the heavy curtains had been drawn against the storm. Light came from a narrow chink at the top and from the side windows of narrow mesh designed to defeat mosquitoes. Benedict and Boniface took up position, guns held in both hands. Edouard cleared his throat before calling: 'Yojo, Yojo, are you there, Yojo?'

Silence.

Edouard tried again: 'Yojo, Yojo, we have come to see if you are okay. Are you all right Yojo?' More silence. 'Are you in the shower, Yojo? Just tell us and we can come back later.' Silence. 'Right, we are going to come in, Yojo, all right?' He nodded to Benedict and Boniface, who moved forward, took one side of the curtains each and drew them back, revealing the bedroom area immediately beyond. It was chaos. Signs of violent destruction were everywhere. The mosquito net had been ripped down. The two campaign chairs lay shattered against the remains of the coffee table, on which brochures advertising Tanzanian holidays could still be seen beneath the shards of wood. The door screens that separated the bedroom area from the bathroom beyond had been ripped from their hinges, which still supported the cross members swinging unevenly in the increased wind. Papers were scattered everywhere. Two large file boxes which the researcher had brought with him on the boat lay on their side, the majority of the contents strewn across the wreckage of the furniture and the bed.

As though driven by some balletic impulse we had all moved slowly into the room. Universally eyes swivelled in search of the same thing. Of Yojo Bo Fang there was no sign. The only noise above the fluttering of paper in the wind was the sound of rain drumming on the thatch. In the distance, thunder rumbled and a flash of sheet lightning lit the sky behind us. Edouard's voice had adopted a hopeless tone.

'Yojo, Yojo, please, Yojo, are you there?'

We moved imperceptibly, shuffling from side to side to improve our individual views, a human instinct as old as horror itself. Suddenly Winnie Sidewinder let out a shriek. 'There, there,' she cried, pointing downwards. 'There, under the bed.' Those who could followed her gaze. On the carpet, protruding from beneath the torn coverlet was the head of Yojo Bo Fang. Only the top of his head was visible. He retained his spectacles, which glinted in the light of the torches now trained on the bedside rug.

'My God,' continued Winnie Sidewinder. 'There he is, there he is. He's been hiding under the bed.'

'I don't think he's conscious,' said Jolyon Downside.

'Stand back,' said Edouard.

Cindy Applebloom pushed herself forward. 'I am a trained nurse,' she said. 'Let me inspect him.'

She moved quickly to the side of the bed and knelt beside Yojo Bo Fang's head.

'Stop, stop,' I cried. 'Don't touch him.'

I was too late. Displaying her obvious prowess, she had taken hold of the head above the ears. Gently she rotated it, and it appeared immediately to assume a life of its own. It turned sideways, then, free of the mosquito net, rolled into the room. Cindy Applebloom screamed and shrank back against the wall.

'My God, my God,' shouted Hiram Sidewinder. 'It's come off. His head's come off.'

Jolyon Downside rushed forward to clasp Cindy Applebloom, narrowly avoiding the head as he did so. There was a loud thud on the floor as Violet Sidewinder dropped her Coca-Cola bottle, which rolled towards the bed. She then immediately vomited. Her mother again clasped her to her bosom and, in the same movement, removed her from the room to the veranda beyond.

'Don't go too far,' said Hiram Sidewinder, 'stay there.'

Briefly there was a pause, a tableau of terror before Edouard attempted to establish control.

'Please, please, everyone, this is a terrible thing but please, let us move quietly out of the room on to the veranda.'

'Where's the rest of him?' said Josh Sidewinder.

'I do not know,' said Edouard, suddenly angry. 'If you will move back I will look under the bed. And please, Miss Applebloom, can you move away and join the others. Boniface, please, have your gun ready in case.' Edouard sank to his knees, took hold of the hanging bed covers and slowly lifted them. With his torch he scanned the floor beneath.

The mind, in crisis, notices ephemera and I distinctly remember noticing Edouard's French accent increase with crisis. The English 'h' disappeared.

''e is not 'ere,' he said, returning to his feet. 'There is nothing. 'e is not 'ere, only the 'ead is 'ere. I will now go and inspect the rest of the 'ut. Please stay here 'ere on the veranda while I do so. Benedict, come with me.'

Leaving a group of guests stunned into silence, Edouard disappeared into the interior of the hut, followed by Benedict, gun at the ready. Within three minutes he returned. 'Nothing,' he announced. 'They break in through the bathroom. There is damage to the walls and blood on the floor but there is nothing else. Now I suggest that we all go back to the lodge together. Please form a line, Benedict first and Boniface at the back. When we are back in the lodge please go upstairs into the library. We will then make a plan.'

As he finished speaking Edouard heard the faintest click. He swung round and confronted John Boxe, whose camera was slung around his neck but whose hand rested on the button.

'What are you doing? What are you doing?'

Boxe looked first at Jolyon Downside. 'Just taking some photographs. That's all.'

'Photographs? You are taking photographs? I demand that you stop immediately.'

'I was told to get as many shots as possible.'

'Who told you to do this? Who told you to do this?'

'My director. He said that it was all good publicity. It's for the film, *Roger*. It's on release next week.'

Edouard became a tower of rage. 'Are you mad? Are you completely stark mad? Can't you see what has happened? A man is dead. All we have is his 'ead and you are taking photographs for *publicity*! I demand you give me the camera at once, at once.'

'This camera,' Boxe said, 'belongs to Robert Bellbottom, the director. He gave it to me specifically for this project. I am not going to give it to you or anyone else.'

'Then give me the film. I demand to have the film.'

'It's a digital camera,' said Jolyon Downside, who had helped Cindy Applebloom back to the group.

'I demand that you stop now, put the cover on the camera.'

Downside nodded to Boxe, who unscrewed the lens. 'I don't have a cover. Will that do?'

Edouard spoke slowly: 'We will see what will do when we have our meeting. We will see. Now please, we will all go back.'

Josh Sidewinder had been looking into the room. Now he said: 'What's going to happen to the head?'

Edouard rounded on him: 'It will remain here until I decide what to do with it.'

Randy Sidewinder joined in: 'But supposing they come back. They already took the body, whoever they are. They could come back for the head.'

I intervened. 'I will bring the head. It can go into one of the file boxes. I would rather do it on my own, so please, Claire and I will follow you to the lodge.'

'You will be alone,' said Edouard.

'We will be careful. I lived here for five years, Edouard. I will be careful.'

When we were alone in the room I picked up a file box, decanted the remaining papers onto the bed and contemplated the head. 'What do you think,' I said, 'I should do about the spectacles?'

I received no reply. Claire was preoccupied at the desk.

'What,' I said again, 'should I do with the spectacles?'

'Sorry?' she said, picking up another sheet of paper.

'Darling,' I said, 'I asked you what I should do about the bloody head. What are you looking at?'

Claire looked up at me. 'Leave the head for the moment. I think you should see these.'

'What? The research papers? I think I have seen enough of those.'

She shook her head. 'These aren't research papers. If they are it is a very strange project.'

I crossed to the desk, on which she had laid out two documents. Both were maps of the Serole National Park. Both bore Chinese script. 'Do you have any Chinese?' I asked, knowing the answer.

'No, but it's not necessary. Look at the maps.'

One of them was a geological map of some age. The other was an aerial photograph of the entire park. Both contained identical lines dividing the park into a number of regions. Several had been cross-hatched in red and green blocks. Taken together the hatched regions extended over one half of the protected area.

I looked across at Claire. 'These could be part of his research data.'

Emphatically she shook her head. 'All of these areas are too remote. Only with extreme difficulty could they be reached from the lodge. If you were able to reach them, there would be neither the time or the resources for research. The chimpanzees in these areas are wild. It would take years, if ever, before they were habituated. But look at the green areas on the photographic surveys. You may need your specs.'

'I don't have them with me.'

Claire shrugged with annoyance. 'This is important. If I am right, this is desperately important.'

I surveyed the desk for signs of lenses or magnifying optics. There were none. I looked back at Claire, who said, 'Oh, take his bloody spectacles, for God's sake. He doesn't need them now. Just be sure to put them in the box.'

'I can't.'

'Of course you can. All right, just don't look.'

Seconds later she reappeared and held the glasses before me. 'They are reading glasses. I thought they were. Now just have a look at those.'

As I arranged the spectacles on my nose I found that they were, indeed, strong reading glasses. Details on the photographic survey were immediately revealed. Claire's finger rested briefly on the green areas and then traced their outline. There was no doubt about it. Within the cross-hatching and directly delineated by its borders, large areas of the forest had disappeared.

'And look at that.' Her finger traced a line following the contours of the mountain.

'It's a road,' I said.

'It's a logging road.'

'Let's have a look at the rest of it.'

In addition to further maps, documents had been scattered across the room which bore Chinese script and diagrams. It was possible on cursory examination to see that none related to primate research. There were also several papers in English. They appeared to contain assessments and valuations.

'Look at this.' Claire held a document before me. It contained a list of native species of timber including teak, tropical oak and mahogany, all found within the Serole forest. I transferred my attention to the head now gazing without spectacles at the ceiling of the hut. As I did so I was aware that Claire had opened a briefcase and was inspecting its contents. She brought another sheaf of papers with her to the desk.

'All Chinese, all company documents of some kind. Not a piece of primate research in sight.' She also turned her attention to the head. 'This guy's a fraud. He wasn't researching primates, he was researching timber. Here in Serole.'

At that moment we heard Edouard, his voice high-pitched with alarm.

'Arthur, Claire, are you all right? For God's sake, what are you doing?' He was standing on the veranda and moving into the bedroom. Behind him I could see Benedict carrying his gun and looking along the shore of the lake. 'What are you doing? I have been worried about you both. Why are you wearing spectacles?'

I attempted to block his view, and Claire picked up a pillow from the bed, but by the time she had placed it over the head it was too late.

'Good God, you are wearing his spectacles. What on earth . . .'

'All right, Edouard, I'll tell you. We have made a discovery. Bo Fang is a fraud.'

'What do you mean he's a fraud? He's a researcher. He comes from the University of something or other.'

'It doesn't matter where he came from.' Claire was now standing behind me. 'It doesn't matter who gave him his papers. He's a logger.'

Edouard's gaze passed between us. 'How do you know?'

73

'Look on the desk. It's all there. The whole Chinese story in black and white.'

Edouard went to the desk, stepping across the pillow. He stayed there for barely three minutes then turned to face us. 'What does this mean?'

'It means,' said Claire, 'that we had an imposter in our group. Worse than that, it means he represented interests that will destroy this park and this place; that are destroying it as we speak.' Her voice fell an octave. 'There is something else. I saw it when I removed the pillow. There it is.' She pointed to the head of the bed, to where the two pillows would have met. An unmistakable pile of chimpanzee dung sat on the linen sheets.

'My God,' said Edouard.

'Dump,' I said.

There was a short silence before Edouard said: 'What do we tell the others? They are waiting for us. We must have another meeting.'

'I think,' I said, 'that we must tell them about this.' I pointed to the defecation. 'We have no choice and, besides, they may already have seen it. As for the identity of our researcher, I suggest we keep it to ourselves for the time being.'

'I agree,' said Edouard.

'So do I,' said Claire.

I picked up the file box and held it out towards Claire. She gathered the head in the pillow and placed both items in the box. She searched briefly for the lid, found it and put it on.

'Let us take the rest,' I said. The three of us gathered together the majority of the scattered papers and put them in the second file box. As I was about to close the lid, Claire stopped, looking at a map.

'Oh my God!' she said.

'What is it?' I said.

'Look, on the top of the document. There are others like it too. Not as clear as this.'

I followed her indication. At the top of the map, on both sides, were the prints of a large ape, similar to a human fingerprint but larger and grained with dirt from the forest floor.

'I have seen this before,' said Edouard.

'So have I,' said Claire. 'We sometimes used to play with them in the old days, give them a book to tear up.'

'I remember. That's what it looked like, just like that.'

Silently Claire put the lid on the remaining box and we set out across the beach towards the lodge, followed by Benedict. The rain had steadily increased and we made slow progress by torchlight carrying the two boxes. As we entered the building, Claire looked at me and froze.

'The spectacles,' she said.

'Oh my God.' As I snatched them from my nose, Hiram Sidewinder emerged from the bar with a large tumbler of whisky.

'Hey,' he said, 'where the hell have you folks been? We've been worried about you. We want to start this meeting. We have got one hell of a lot to discuss.'

As we climbed the stairs I managed to stuff the spectacles into my inside jacket pocket. We reached the library level, set down our respective file boxes and joined the meeting.

CHAPTER 10

When the meeting reconvened it was barely an hour and a half since we had broken off in the search for Violet Sidewinder. She was now firmly within the party, sitting between her parents with a new bottle of Coca-Cola. Edouard assumed his role as chair and began in a tone of calm authority.

'Ladies and gentlemen, first let us deal with personal matters. Despite the awful events that have taken place I am aware that none of you have eaten this evening. It is now gone eight o'clock and I therefore propose that this emergency meeting should be kept to a minimum. I have asked that food should be served at nine o'clock, by which time we will have made all the necessary arrangements and precautions.'

There was a general murmur of assent before he continued, 'Now, it cannot be denied that we have all suffered a severe shock, a most dreadful event which has cost the life of one of our guests. The circumstances of that death will, in due course, be the subject of serious and detailed examination.'

'Ah, hell,' said Hiram Sidewinder, 'hell, Edouard, why don't you get to the point? We have had a murder committed. A murder. Furthermore, it looks increasingly likely that this murder was carried out by a mad ape, probably leading other mad apes, and here is one thing that you may not have noticed but I certainly did. On the bed at the scene of the murder there was a great heap of ape shit.'

'We noticed that,' said Edouard, 'we know it was there.'

'Well, hell,' said Hiram Sidewinder, 'this heap of ape shit fits exactly with what you were saying before. What Arthur here was telling us about this aberrant ape. This is his signature. As they say in crime movies, this is his MO. His *modus operandi*. Also, the severed head. Arthur has told us that this ape tore the head off another ape barely three days ago. To my mind this proves conclusively that the same ape was responsible. Furthermore, it means we can discount Muslim extremists, although, in my view, my wife made a very good case, but this ape shit has now put the matter beyond doubt. I am sorry, I do not want to hijack the meeting but it is now clear that this Dump must be shot and shot quickly.'

Hiram Sidewinder sat back, took a long pull from his whisky and acknowledged a smattering of applause from his family. Edouard tried to re-establish control.

'Mr Sidewinder, I acknowledge that there is a compelling case to be made for urgent action but . . .'

'If I may just interrupt,' said Jolyon Downside from his seat on the sofa, closely pressed against Cindy Applebloom, 'is not the first priority for us to leave the lodge at the earliest possible moment and by whatever means is available? May we know whether you have managed to establish radio or telephone contact with the outside world, with the authorities?'

'I was going to come to that,' said Edouard. 'I have, of course, attempted to contact the park authorities by telephone and, indeed, anyone else with whom we can establish radio contact. However, as you are well aware, there is an electric storm over the mountains and the weather has got markedly worse. At the moment radio and telephone contact is very poor. I have, indeed, attempted to put out an emergency Mayday signal but I have no way of knowing whether it has been received or understood. As to evacuation, the lodge, as you know, has no airstrip. The nearest is thirty kilometres away through thick jungle. There is a helicopter pad ten kilometres to the north for use in emergencies only. Except in the gravest emergency no helicopter would fly over the mountains in these conditions. That leaves embarkation by boat. There is a storm raging over the lake. This is by no means unusual. When there is foul weather like this it centres on the lake. To embark in a boat at the present time would be unthinkable. Tomorrow is a possibility but only at considerable risk. Which brings me to our immediate precautions. I suggest that we should all move into the lodge; specifically, into the upper area of the lodge where we now are. I suggest that the Sidewinder family should occupy the northern end over there. There are abundant couches and cushions upon which you can make yourselves very comfortable. I suggest that Mr Downside and Miss Applebloom should take the other end of the library. Again, the day furniture may be converted into a comfortable sleeping area. I myself will sleep downstairs in the lodge and also Arthur and Claire can sleep in the bar area. Benedict and Boniface will remain with us. They are both armed, as you can see, and will be constantly vigilant throughout the night. Before we eat this evening we may all make individual visits to our huts, accompanied either by Benedict or Boniface, to collect what essential belongings we require. That leaves only, I think, John Boxe, who, I am delighted to say, is no longer taking photographs.'

Jolyon Downside intervened. 'John can stay in our part of the lodge, that is not a problem. But I have a suggestion to make which may assist in communication. Cindy and I have a satellite phone. We have it for the transmission of publicity material for the film. So far communication has been sporadic but we will continue to try and will let you know if we succeed.'

Edouard was not pleased. 'I am sorry, I was not aware that such a phone existed. May I request that communication with it is kept to a bare minimum? The events that have happened here may be open to serious misinterpretation if based on limited information. If you do manage to establish clear communication, please let me know at once.'

Hiram Sidewinder was sitting like a man deeply restrained. Now he burst forth. 'Hell, that may be okay for you, Edouard, but it is sure as hell not okay for me. What we are doing here is adopting a defensive role, sheltering behind two AK-47s which I guarantee have not been fired in anger for twenty years. We have seen enough to know that this Dump is dangerous. He's an ape but he's a dangerous ape.' He finished his whisky and sat forward in his chair. 'What we must do, Edouard, we must go on the offensive. If we can't get an air force or navy in here we must go out there and do it ourselves. This aberrant ape must be stopped. The time has come, Edouard, to unlock the guns, my guns, real guns. We don't know how many apes this Dump has persuaded to join him but, judging from the noises they make, there may be hundreds. If we are attacked by hundreds of chimpanzees what chance do we stand with two peashooters in the hands of those with no experience? I know the rules. I know, Edouard, that you can't release those guns *except in an emergency* and this is an emergency, big time. This Dump needs to be stopped.'

Edouard began, 'I am afraid . . .' but was interrupted by Jolyon Downside.

'I must say,' said the actor, 'that I think Hiram is right. At least we should issue the firearms in order that we may be ready. I do not agree with an "offensive" but I do agree with taking sensible precautions. This is obviously an emergency and we should treat it as such. Desperate times need desperate measures.'

Edouard looked directly at me. 'Well,' he said, 'what do you think?'

I took a deep breath. 'I think Mr Sidewinder has a point. Let us issue the firearms on the strict instruction that they are to be used only in defence.'

Jolyon Downside chimed in again. 'I think that is very sensible, very sensible indeed. If I may offer my services, I know a little of firearms. I was in the Combined Cadet Force at school.'

'Hell, no,' said Hiram Sidewinder, 'that's kind of you, Mr Downside, but my whole family is skilled in the use of weapons. We each have our own firearm. Why, even little Violet has got her 2.2 and shot a buffalo down in the Selous. She didn't manage to kill it, of course, I had to finish it off with my 407. So, if you don't mind, we'll take the firearms. Together with the staff boys we have eight guns, which should be more than enough to deter this Dump.'

Edouard was silent. I watched the conflict within him. I could feel it in myself. Guns had never been carried by visitors to Serole, the idea was anathema. On the other hand they provided the means to rid ourselves of Dump, to return to an idyllic existence. Finally Edouard shrugged and stood. 'Very well. Unless anyone else has anything to contribute I will get the box. Benedict and Boniface will escort you to your rooms. Be sure to bring rain gear with you. I suggest that we eat in half an hour.'

Claire and I were the first to visit our hut and afterwards, while the rest of the preparations were made, we sat in a quiet corner of the bar drinking stiff gins. 'Well,' I said, 'you obviously think I've made a mistake.'

'Not a mistake, but I think it is dangerous. Arming the Sidewinders does not fill me with a sense of wellbeing.'

'Nor me, but it is done. There is something else worrying you?'

Claire took a long draught of her drink, put the glass down, looked straight at me and said: 'There is. I will tell you what it is, but what I am going to say will sound quite mad. You and I have worked together with chimpanzees and other primates for twenty years. What I am going to say is heresy of the worst kind. It would be rejected as academic lunacy.'

'Go on.'

'What if our bogus researcher, our Chinese logger, didn't come from China or wherever on a research trip. What if he came from the illegal logging areas shown on the map? We only know that he joined the boat at the edge of the park. What if he was recognised? What if they knew he was here?'

'By *they* you mean the chimpanzees?'

'Exactly.'

'But that is crazy. Chimpanzees are clever but they are not strategic. There may have been all kinds of conflict in the logging areas.'

'I believe that there has been. I have heard that chimps have been shot, perhaps even many of them.'

'But to pursue him here to Serole would require planning, strategic planning.'

'All right, but supposing they knew who he was and found out that he was here?'

'Find out? How would they find out that he was here?'

'God knows.' She thought for a moment. 'They read the maps.'

'Read the maps? Chimpanzees don't read maps.'

'Their fingerprints were on them.'

'But that is coincidence.'

'Coincidence when they ransacked his room? Why did they ransack the room?'

'God knows. Destructive impulse? Same destructive urge that pulled his head off?'

'I will put it all to you,' Claire said. 'I believe that this is Ronald Dump. I believe that he is alive and I believe that he has succeeded in doing something that no ape has ever been known to do before. To assemble his own following from among the mountain troupes. The wild chimpanzees.'

'But how could he do that?'

'The Chinese loggers, the destruction of their habitat, the threat to their lives – there is a dreadful anger. What if Dump has somehow persuaded them that he could lead them?'

'But he's mad. In chimp terms he is a violent psychopath.'

'Precisely.'

'And why us? Why should they threaten us, here in Serole? We have never harmed the chimpanzees, never done anything but study them, befriend them.'

'But we have not protected them. When the loggers came, we did not protect them and we are, after all, human. Even the Sidewinders are human.'

I finished my drink in silence, staring out over the lake, conscious that Claire was watching me. Edouard called us to the dinner table. As we rose, she said: 'You think I'm mad, don't you?'

'I don't know,' I said, 'I really don't know.'

82

CHAPTER 11

By nine o'clock the entire party, accompanied by Benedict and Boniface, had visited their huts and returned to the lodge with assorted luggage. This they distributed to the areas which had been designated by Edouard and began the process of creating temporary accommodation. Jolyon Downside and Cindy Applebloom moved two sofas together, upon which they spread the sheets and duvet that they had brought from the hut. A little further away John Boxe was accommodated on the floor with cushions removed from the library chairs. At the other end of the library, the Sidewinders made similar provision, instinctively moving the sofas and chairs into a circle which provided at least the illusion of security. Following their visit to their hut the Sidewinders had become practically unrecognisable. All of them had changed into army fatigues and boots which appeared suitable for military operations. Even Violet Sidewinder looked entirely fit for battle. This, I assumed, represented the Sidewinders in full hunting regalia, ready for animal warfare of whatever kind. Claire and I had made our home in the area behind the bar and Edouard had colonised the far end of the lodge, close to the serving area, whence Erasmus now emerged carrying a tray of soup which he ladled into the plates set out on the table. Unfortunately, places had been laid for the Bellingham sisters and Yojo Bo Fang which remained vacant when the rest of the party assembled.

'Shouldn't we clear those away?' said Randy Sidewinder. 'We know they won't be coming to dinner and it looks kind of sad having the empty chairs.'

Edouard nodded to Erasmus and at the vacant places. When he had served the soup, he collected the settings on the tray and departed. As he left the room, Benedict and Boniface entered carrying the metal gun box which contained the Sidewinders' weapons. This was placed on a coffee table close to the bar.

'Thank you,' said Edouard. 'I suggest, for the time being, you take up post at either end of the library where you can see the entire beach.'

As the party commenced to eat the soup, a semblance of normality returned. Josh Sidewinder enquired of Jolyon Downside whether he had ever been in any war movies. Downside replied that, when much younger, he had played a German officer with a monocle in a film about the unsuccessful assassination of Hitler.

'It was practically a non-speaking role,' he said. 'I appeared only in the room where the planning meeting took place and the bomb was planted. I stood next to the Führer by the map table while he demonstrated a massive offensive on the Eastern Front.'

'Hell,' said Josh Sidewinder, 'that must have been fascinating.'

'Unfortunately not. My only line delivered direct to Hitler himself was to say "*Ach so, mein Führer,*" just before the explosion took place. As you know, Hitler was unharmed, but I lost a leg.'

'Hell,' said Hiram Sidewinder, 'did that actually happen?'

'I haven't the faintest idea. I only know that there was a brief linked shot of the Führer being helped unharmed from the wreckage while I was carried away on a stretcher with one leg. That is to say that I had one leg. Curiously I still had the monocle and an expression of noble suffering. That's what it said in the directions. "Noble suffering." While on the stretcher I did originally have another line – "Will I still be able to go to the Eastern Front?" – but it was cut.'

'And how about you?' Winnie Sidewinder had turned to Cindy Applebloom. 'Were you in any movies about war or conflict?'

'No, I am afraid not. My agent once put me forward to be raped in Greece but casting said I was too tall.'

'Hell,' said Hiram Sidewinder, 'you don't seem too tall to be raped. How tall are you, five seven, five eight?'

Cindy Applebloom directed a cold glance towards Sidewinder before saying: 'Five seven and a half. That is apparently too tall for a Greek peasant.'

Jolyon Downside intervened. 'I think we really should come back to the present crisis. I believe that the rain is stopping. The wind has fallen and I have heard no thunder for an hour or so. It may well be that the storm has passed.'

Seated at the head of the table, Edouard nodded. 'I think you are right. The lake is still very rough and it would be unwise to attempt to cross by boat tonight. However, at first light we will assess the situation, by which time I may have heard from base about the helicopter. In the meantime, let us continue as normally as possible.'

As though on cue, Erasmus re-entered with a tray to clear the plates. Randy Sidewinder rose and walked to the bar. 'I'll get another two bottles of wine,' he said. 'Anyone want anything else?'

No one replied. Erasmus finished gathering the plates. As he passed Edouard he bent down and spoke softly into his ear before leaving the room. Edouard remained for a moment in obvious contemplation. He then pushed back his chair and said: 'I must attend to something before we have our main course. Arthur, do you think you could come with me? You may be able to help.'

I rose and followed him out of the lodge. When we got to the beach it was clear that the rain had indeed stopped. The odd drop fell from the brightening sky. The silhouette of the mountains now appeared black and motionless above us. The wind had also dropped and we quickly covered the sixty metres to the edge of the jungle, behind which, barely concealed, was the kitchen and the staff quarters. As we walked Edouard said quietly, 'I think we have a problem with the staff.'

CHAPTER 12

When we entered the kitchen I saw that the entire staff was assembled around the huge centre table. Erasmus and Coleridge I knew well. Four male kitchen staff I recognised from my time at the lodge and also two of their wives who were employed to help in the kitchen area. Four of the women who attended to the huts and the cleaning were known to me: Purity, Alice, Mary and Angela, all smiling at me from the end of the table. Otherwise the group was impassive, serious and radiating concern. In the centre of the table on a sheet of newspaper lay a tin water bottle bearing the logo of the lodge, and a desert boot. The top of the water bottle was missing and the tin itself was dented in a number of places. No one sat down. Edouard spoke first.

'Erasmus,' he said, 'you wanted to see us and here we are. Can we speak English? You all know Arthur, who has returned to the lodge after a long time in England. I suspect that his Swahili is very rusty.'

Erasmus nodded and began. 'Bwana,' he said, 'we are all very worried. We know about the Chinaman. Benedict and Boniface have told us. That is very bad. But that is not our main concern. We know that Moses has gone missing, has not come back and neither have the English women.'

Edouard nodded. 'That is correct, yes.'

'But now this has happened.' Erasmus pointed to the objects

87

on the table. 'These belong to Moses, his bottle and his boot. One hour ago they were thrown here, outside the door. We did not see where they came from but there is much movement in the trees. I think there are many chimpanzees in the forest, some here, some deep, but they hide and then we hear them calling. It is not a call we have heard before. It is different. Like a song, like a chant. It is not like any sound I have heard before. It the same with all of us. Some of us have been here many years, many years, Mr Edouard, but we do not hear this before. Also, Moses and this.' He pointed again to the centre of the table and all eyes irresistibly moved to the compelling evidence of violence and theft.

Edouard spoke quietly to Erasmus but, in reality, addressing the whole meeting. 'What do you think it means?'

'We think Moses is dead and the ladies too. How dead we don't know, but dead. I have known Moses for twenty-five years. He is my friend and our best guide. If alive he would come back.'

All eyes turned to Edouard, who stood silently contemplating the table. Eventually, he said: 'I think you are right. There cannot be another explanation. Let me tell you the decisions that we have made. I would have told you later this evening but you can know now. We have made arrangements to evacuate the lodge. All our guests have moved into the main building. The storm has now passed and it may be possible to evacuate first thing in the morning. You must all move into this kitchen and stay here. It is a good building with barred windows and roof. If it is necessary to move food and supplies between the kitchen and the lodge, then it must be done with either Benedict or Boniface as escort. As you know, they have their firearms. I have asked for a helicopter to come tomorrow, I do not know when, but I have asked. As early as possible we will load the guests on to the boat and leave for Akawi. We will need Benedict to drive the boat and Boniface will remain here. You should also know that I have issued the firearms belonging to a number of the guests. Four members of the party are armed and can use their weapons if absolutely necessary. Now I suggest that we should eat our meal and then we will wait until the morning.'

At the far end of the table Erasmus was shaking his head. 'No, bwana, I am sorry,' he said. 'I think we should not stay. We should go now. We do not have much time. These chimpanzees, bad chimpanzees, are very close. This is why they throw these. They tell us they are very close. They tell us that Moses is dead. And the English ladies and the Chinaman. And there are many, many of them. In the rain and the storm, we have not heard them in the trees but now, if you listen, you can hear them. They are all along the shore. Some, I think, have entered the huts which your guests have left. We are surrounded by the forest and by the lake. We think we must go now. We all think this.'

When he finished there was a general murmur of agreement before Edouard said: 'Erasmus, I hear what you say and I understand, but there are twelve of you here. With Benedict and Boniface, that is fourteen. We have nine guests including Arthur and Claire, that makes twenty-three people plus myself. The boat holds a maximum of twelve people including the driver and one member to crew. That is in good, calm weather. We have a storm out there. It is better now but it will be worse out on the lake. I will not be responsible for launching the boat. For the moment we are safer here. Whatever has happened to . . . the others.'

'Bwana,' said Erasmus, 'we cannot defend the kitchen if they attack. They will tear out the windows. The roof is made of tin.

They will lift it easily. We have no weapons, just these.' He held up a meat cleaver and a frying pan. 'How long do you think I can fight a chimpanzee with this?' He waved the frying pan over his head and brought it down on to the table top.

I had known Erasmus for fifteen years. A kind old Tanzanian, brought up in the traditions of the Nyerere government, non-tribal, non-violent. Now, with the cleaver in his hand, I saw a man I did not know. I thought, 'It is our lodge but it is his country.'

'You,' he said, 'now have many weapons in the lodge. You have the hunting people trained to kill. Here,' he gestured across the kitchen, 'we only have ourselves and we are in the jungle.'

Edouard looked straight at Erasmus and spoke softly, one man of experience speaking directly to another. 'Erasmus, you have worked here as long as I have, twenty-five years. You have lived with the chimpanzees. You know them, you know their families, you know the troupe. Have you ever felt threatened before? Ever felt afraid? This is surely not the time . . .'

Erasmus interrupted him, his voice rising with conviction. 'No, bwana, no, Mr Edouard, no. These are not like our chimpanzees. These are not the same. These are not Serole chimpanzees. These are different. These chimpanzees are from the forest, from the jungle, from far, far away and there are many, many of them. And they are bad, bad. They sound bad and they are bad.'

'They are the same.'

'No, Mr Edouard, they are not the same. Something has made them mad. Something has made them bad.' He paused heavily and then said, 'Dump. It is Dump. He has made them mad. You know Dump, Mr Edouard. He is bad, very bad chimpanzee and he make them all bad, like him, like him.'

Edouard held up a weak hand. 'Dump is dead.'

'No, Mr Edouard, no. Dump is not dead. Dump is alive and out there. Moses knew Dump was alive. He told us he had not seen him but he had seen the signs and he had seen what he can do. Moses knew that Dump was alive and now Moses is dead. Moses is dead and English ladies and the Chinese man, they are all dead and if we stay we also will be dead.' There was a very long pause before Erasmus continued. 'And, Mr Edouard, bwana, you know, you know Dump is not dead. Dump is not dead because you tell the guests that Dump is not dead. Arthur, you tell them that Dump is not dead.'

I answered for Edouard. 'You are right, Erasmus, I believe he is alive. I did believe he was dead and I believed I had killed him. Whether he has caused this . . . rebellion, this change in the forest chimps, I don't know. It has never happened before. People have studied chimpanzees for two centuries and this behaviour has never been observed before. But you are right. I think he is alive and he is capable of terrible things.'

Erasmus said, 'Thank you.'

Edouard said, 'Very well, let me tell you what I will do. I repeat there can be no question of the boat being used tonight. There are too many people and the weather is treacherous. Tomorrow, all being well, we can begin to depart. I must insist that the guests leave first. If the weather has improved they can leave at seven o'clock. In two and a half hours they can be in Akawi. If they disembark and refuel quickly the boat can be back by one o'clock. Our guests will go but I will remain here. We will evacuate everyone else at one o'clock. That includes all of the staff. The helicopter may then have landed but it is incapable of taking more than three passengers and will be ten kilometres into the jungle. I suggest that everyone waits for the boat. As for tonight, Erasmus, I would ask you to serve dinner, protected by Benedict and Boniface. Afterwards both of them will come here to the kitchen with their weapons. They will remain here throughout the night and you must make arrangements for sleeping as best you can. They are both armed, so you will not need cleavers or frying pans. After a day or two I will arrange a full complement of Tanzanian Park Rangers to return fully armed. Further boats can be commissioned from different parts of the lake. We will resolve this matter, once and for all, and return to the civilised way of life that we had before. If it is, indeed, Dump who is responsible for these . . . murders, then he will be hunted down and despatched. I hope, Erasmus, that that satisfies you.'

If it did, it was not immediately apparent. Erasmus shook his head. 'No boat?'

'No boat,' said Edouard firmly, 'you must see that that is suicide. Now Arthur and I can risk going back alone. I will ensure that Benedict and Boniface are here to escort you with the food.' His tone softened. 'I know, Erasmus, that this is a crisis and terrible things have happened but it will be resolved and it will be all right. If it is Dump he will be beaten. Power such as his never prevails.'

It was, I thought, an over-grand rhetorical flourish but it appeared to have the sympathy of at least some of his audience.

As we walked back, he turned to me and said: 'That was all right wasn't it?' But as I started to answer I saw that he was not looking at me but over my shoulder into the middle distance, into the jungle. 'Christ,' he said.

CHAPTER 13

I turned and followed his gaze. I saw them immediately. Erasmus had been right. The wind and the storm had concealed any other movement in the high branches. Now that both had subsided they became clearly visible. Dark shapes swinging and moving, occasionally silhouetted against the sky. As they moved the soft familiar noises of chimpanzees reached us on the ground like soft exhalations of breath. *Hoo, hoo, hoo.* As our eyes became accustomed we saw the shaking and swaying replicated high up on to the foothills of the mountain.

'Christ,' said Edouard again, 'how many do you think?'

'I can't tell,' I said, 'it's almost impossible. Forty? Fifty? They are not ours, are they?'

Edouard shook his head. 'Definitely not. That is not the behaviour of our chimps. They would let us know they were there. Some certainly would be on the ground even at night.'

While we watched the trees suddenly became still. I was to tell Claire later that it appeared as though there was a regimental precision. There was a brief moment of silence before the organised, orchestrated calling began again. A hunting call but delivered in unison. A rising chant like a whistle delivered from the back of the throat. Then it ended with a single abrupt note. '*Humph!*' As soon as it had finished it started again, the same long exhalation rising to a scream before the sudden '*Humph!*'

'Good God,' said Edouard, 'have you ever heard that? Anything like it?'

I shook my head, still staring at the upper forest. 'Never, never. We must go back.'

Without consciously doing so we found ourselves running over the soft sand. The space between ourselves and the lights of the lodge was barely fifty metres but in the sand our strides became desperately slow, like running in a dream, terror and paralysis linked together. As we reached the threshold we both instinctively stopped. Public panic was to be avoided.

The whole remaining party were sitting on the sofas and chairs overlooking the sea. Hiram Sidewinder rose up, as did Jolyon Downside.

'Hell,' said the American, 'where have you folks been? We were going to send out a search party, then that goddamn noise started. Also Mr Boxe here says that he has seen movement in the trees, not the wind or the storm but animals, big animals. Did you see any of that?'

'Yes, we did,' said Edouard, looking at me as he spoke.

'Well, what did you make of it? What the hell's going on out there? And another thing: the huts, our huts, the ones that we left, you know they have a bell system for room service, cleaning and that?'

Edouard nodded.

'Well, they keep on going off and we know there is no one there, no one. There is even ringing coming from the Chinaman's room and we know he ain't there, don't we? There is only his head and that's over there.' Hiram Sidewinder pointed to the two file boxes at the far end of the bar. He frowned. 'Don't you think we ought to do something about that head? I mean, I don't like to think of it sitting there. Have you got a refrigerator we could put it in, a deep freeze? When this gets sorted out the forensic people are going to want to have a look at it.'

'Yes,' said Edouard, preoccupied, 'I will tell Erasmus to put it in the deep freeze.'

'I think that would be wise,' said Hiram Sidewinder. 'It's okay now but if it gets hot tomorrow, we won't be here but it could still smell a bit.'

'Fine, fine,' said Edouard, 'it will be done. I have asked Erasmus to bring the rest of our dinner but I must get Benedict and Boniface to fetch him. Perhaps everyone could come back to the table.'

'Hell, that's fine,' said Hiram Sidewinder, 'we ought to have something to eat. If these guys, Benedict and Boniface, are going to be moving backwards and forwards to the kitchen quarters then we need our guns, Edouard. They are over there in their box and I think you have the key.'

Edouard looked at me, then at Claire and Jolyon Downside. 'Very well,' he said, 'we will get them out, but before they are even loaded we must establish quite clear rules of engagement.'

'Rules of engagement? Hell, that's fine by me.'

Edouard felt in the pocket of his safari jacket and produced a ring with two keys.

'There are two here,' he said.

'That's right,' said Hiram Sidewinder, 'there's one for the inner and one for the outer box. That box has come all the way from Memphis, Tennessee. Down South we take gun security seriously. You got guns, you keep 'em locked up, and I've got a hell of a lot of guns.'

'Very well,' said Edouard, handing over the keyring. 'Arthur,' he said to me, 'would you go and get Benedict? He's down at the far end. I will tell Boniface to escort our dinner.'

Before the main course arrived, the Sidewinders opened the box. Driven by a human curiosity we moved towards the case as the contents were revealed. There were six guns of various sizes. One by one they emerged from the box and were distributed to their owners. Josh and Randy Sidewinder, the twins, received identical weapons. Large, smooth rifles with protruding magazines, these were immediately followed by telescopic sights which both brothers applied to the top of their guns. They made identical and near-simultaneous clicks. Hiram Sidewinder held up his own gun.

'The 407,' he said, pointing it across the lake. 'This one you see has a bolt action. That's because the ammunition is so large it is more likely to jam, whereas the smaller weapons are semi-automatic.'

Winnie Sidewinder's rifle was a little smaller but similar to that of her sons. 'Semi-automatic,' she said, 'one shot per second. Twenty in the magazine.'

'Here you are, darling,' said Hiram Sidewinder, handing a smaller weapon to Violet. 'Don't you look good with that? Hey, come over here, Mr Boxe, and get a picture of my Violet with her 2.2. She shot a buffalo with it in the Selous. Didn't kill it so I had to follow it into the bush and finish it off and that's what it's all about, ain't it, darling? Finish the kill, that's how they've been brought up. Finish the kill.'

While John Boxe took photographers of Violet Sidewinder, gun cradled in the crook of her arm, the main course, coq au vin, arrived escorted by Benedict and Boniface. Erasmus served the meal to a silent table.

The staff were about to leave when Hiram Sidewinder intervened. 'Hey, Edouard, I think if Benedict and Boniface are going back to the kitchen we need to post sentries until they return.'

'Hiram, I really don't think that is necessary. They will be gone only a matter of minutes.'

'Minutes is all they need, don't you see? When an animal kills, he kills real quick. Hell, I've seen a pack of wild dogs bring down an adult wildebeest. Sure, they chase it for a while but then the lead dog (they take it in rotation you know), he gets right up there behind the wildebeest, which starts kicking wildly because he knows that the attack is coming. Then the lead dog, he goes straight for the balls and that old wildebeest, one minute he is running along and the next minute he ain't got no balls and that slows him down. I don't know why but it slows him down and then it is so quick, so quick.'

'Could we talk about something else?' said Cindy Applebloom.

Jolyon Downside, beside her, nodded. 'Yes, perhaps we could.'

'The only point I'm trying to make is that when an animal decides he is going to kill, he kills. He doesn't come in and say, "Would you mind finishing your coq au vin." He goes right in, right in. I know a bit about animal behaviour. When you have killed as many animals as I have, you know a lot about animal behaviour, so the only point I am making is that if we don't have any sentries while we are eating our main course, those apes, those Dumps could be in here tearing our balls off before you can say knife.'

'I'll go and be a sentry,' said Cindy Applebloom, 'if that makes you feel better. Where do you think I ought to stand?'

'Hell, no. That's not a job for a woman. I wouldn't even let

Winnie do that job. That's a job for a man. Randy, why don't you take up a position just out there on the beach, where you can see both ways, and be sure to let us know the first thing you see. Then when Benedict and Boniface come back, you can eat your food.'

'I think I should tell you,' said Edouard, 'that I have asked Benedict and Boniface to remain in the kitchen tonight for the safety of the staff.'

'The staff?' said Winnie Sidewinder. 'What about us? I suppose now that we have our own firearms . . .'

'Sure,' said Hiram Sidewinder, 'but we can't damn well use them. We have got to go through all this rules of engagement stuff. And another thing we have got to talk about; how do we make this place defensible given a mass attack from the jungle led by this Dump? Where are we going to draw our lines? If you want my opinion this place is pretty goddamn indefensible. It is like Rorke's Drift, did you ever see that movie about Rorke's Drift? They tipped over the wagons to give themselves a firing step. My God, that was a good movie. Now, of course, they were Zulus, not chimpanzees but the same applies.'

I thought that the time had come to help Edouard. 'Mr Sidewinder, Hiram,' I said, 'I think we need to keep a sense of proportion. No one is anticipating a mass attack. Chimpanzees may occasionally be fierce. In the case of Dump, it is true, I believe him to be aberrant and dangerous. But a mass attack, a mass movement of any kind requires strategy and organisation. Chimpanzees are not Zulus, they are incapable of such organisation, Dump or no Dump.'

'So you say,' said Hiram Sidewinder. 'You told us that chimpanzees were essentially harmless, that they had never been known to attack human beings. But if you are right, then what the hell is in that goddamn box and how did it get there?'

'I have already agreed that there is an aberrant chimpanzee, perhaps even more than one.'

'Hell,' interrupted Hiram Sidewinder, 'it would take more than one to tear his head off. You have got to have someone to hold the other end so that's at least two. And who's ringing those goddamn bells? There are eight huts out there all jingle-jangle. If that's not organisation, tell me what is. All calling for room service at the same time.'

'I acknowledge that something very unusual, something unprecedented may be happening but it stops short of mass action.'

'Okay, okay,' Winnie Sidewinder intervened, 'okay. I'll try and be a voice of reason. Maybe we are not anticipating a mass attack but even if it is just something unusual, we have got to look at this lodge and decide what is defensible and what is not and who is going to defend it. Then we have got to decide what are the rules of engagement, so why don't we finish our dessert, which I see has been put on the sideboard over there, and then replenish our drinks and walk around and decide exactly that.'

'A very sensible idea,' said Jolyon Downside. 'Can I get you a pudding, Winnie?'

'Why Jolyon, thank you. I'll have one of the chocolate ones in the front.'

CHAPTER 14

After the pudding, for the next hour Hiram Sidewinder followed Edouard around the lodge. Behind him came Winnie Sidewinder with a clipboard and pencil. 'Reconnaissance,' said Hiram Sidewinder. 'Time spent on reconnaissance is seldom wasted.'

'Were you actually ever in the army?' Edouard enquired as they mounted the stairs.

'I was in the Royal Marine Corps. I was a dentist in the Royal Marine Corps. Did I ever see combat? Hell, no. Did I see the results of combat? Yes, I saw some when our boys came home from the Iraq War, but mainly it was the usual thing, pulling and filling, pulling and filling. I've got a lot more sophisticated since then.'

At the end of the tour, the entire party assembled around the dining-room table. Hiram Sidewinder helped himself to a large glass of whisky. The Sidewinder twins drank beer and Violet Sidewinder had a bottle of Coke. The firearms had been leant against the sideboard in descending order of size and lethality.

'Right,' said Hiram Sidewinder, 'the first thing is that I have identified the perfect lookout, the point of advantage. It is upstairs on the balcony which overlooks the beach. Someone, armed, should be there at all times. Randy, if you would.'

As Randy Sidewinder climbed the stairs, checking his telescopic sight, Edouard intervened. 'Hiram, Mr Sidewinder, before you start we must have some rules here. I know that you are only doing your best and you have all of our interests at heart but there must be rules as to the use of firearms. In particular I must insist that no chimpanzees are to be shot or shot at without express permission from me or from Arthur. Many chimpanzees, out there, we have known for many years. They are our friends. I know all of them, Arthur knows most of them. It is essential that no harm comes to them.'

Hiram Sidewinder looked at Edouard, eyes narrowed over his whisky glass. 'What happens if there is a night attack, a sudden sortie while you and Arthur are asleep? Can you recognise your chimpanzees, your *friends*, in the darkness? Hell, we could be overwhelmed before we have a chance.'

From the far side of the table I saw Cindy Applebloom close her eyes. Jolyon Downside captured her hand and placed it securely on his thigh.

I supported Edouard. 'Hiram,' I said, 'I may not be any good with guns but I am an expert in primate behaviour. As you know, I think what you suggest is highly fanciful. In reality, impossible. Chimpanzees have never been known to behave in such a way since research began.' I raised a hand to pre-empt interruption. 'However, even if this event, this pattern of behaviour, was credible, I can tell you that chimpanzees do not hunt at night. They are like us, they sleep at night, together, in fact, in groups. When they hunt they hunt in the day and they hunt monkeys, colobus and red-tailed monkeys. This is carried out entirely in the trees, not on the ground. Of course, there are unanswered questions. Of course, something serious is happening but we should not anticipate a complete change in primate behaviour. This is unthinkable.'

Winnie Sidewinder turned towards me. 'Haven't we been here before? Don't you accept that things have happened which break all your rules? Have we seen any of your "friends", the civilised, habituated chimpanzees? No, we have not and you have heard them, *we have all heard them*, that terrible screaming and chanting at night. That is not the noise of families sleeping.'

'Mrs Sidewinder, Winnie . . .' I began.

'And how many are there? How many are out there in the forest making that noise? How many are in the huts ringing for room service? Fifty, a hundred, hundreds? Tell us because we all need to know.'

I paused and looked at Edouard, then shook my head. 'I don't know. I simply do not know.'

'In that case,' said Hiram Sidewinder, 'we must be prepared. Early tomorrow morning we will all be on a boat and safe. In the meantime, we must be prepared. I have here a diagram indicating our points of weakness and our points of strength.' Sidewinder spread his diagram upon the table. Unwillingly I leant forward to see it, as did the remainder of the group with the exception of Cindy Applebloom, who remained with her eyes tight closed and her hand reassuringly on the thigh of Jolyon Downside.

'This here,' said Hiram Sidewinder, 'is the lake side of the lodge. It is almost all open and completely indefensible. However, I am told by Edouard here that there is strong canvas sheeting that can be secured down and zipped up. It is there to protect from the weather. The canvas sheets should be drawn down and secured immediately. When that is done, with the exception of the floor above, we can ignore that side of the building. Here, to the rear, the forest-facing side of the building is open to the beach. The jungle is approximately fifty metres away. This is undoubtedly our weakest point. In my view this should be blocked immediately with as much furniture as we can find. This dining-room table will have to go, I'm afraid, and the sideboard. I know, I know it is not much but it creates a barrier, a psychological barrier. It says, "This is our land, this belongs to us. Here we stand." Hell, even a primate can understand that.'

I looked across the table at Claire, who rolled her eyes gently towards the ceiling before closing them.

'Then we have either end of the building. The bar is open where it faces the beach and from there you can see all the guest huts. This is another weak point and similar precautions should be taken. And, finally, here we have the far end of the lodge and the service area that has been designated as the sleeping quarters for Edouard, Arthur and Claire. That area is closed off by a wall. It consists, Edouard tells me, of wooden planking and thatch. We can assume that area to be safe.

'Now, upstairs.' He allowed the first sheet of paper to roll up, revealing beneath it a rough plan of the library area above. 'This area is completely enclosed by thatch which extends well below the floor. Again, it could be torn up but, for these purposes, we will assume that it is safe. There are two large balconies, one facing the lake and the other the forest. To the lake side there is again strong canvas sheeting which can be lowered. To the forest side it is open and this, again, is a weak point. The top of the balustrade is approximately three or four metres from the ground. Can you tell us, Arthur, with your expertise, can you tell us how long it would take a chimpanzee to climb to that height?'

All eyes turned to me and I said: 'Seconds, possibly two at the most.'

'Hell,' said Hiram Sidewinder, 'they can climb that high in that time?'

'In one bound. These are the greatest trapeze artists on earth.'

'My God, that is serious, that is serious.'

I saw Cindy Applebloom, eyes still tight shut, take a sudden inhalation of breath.

'Well, that's going to need more thought. Now I come to the firearms. For as long as Benedict and Boniface are not with us, we have four powerful guns. In addition, I have in a case over there a handgun, a Smith and Wesson. It is my own handgun and I carry it in the bush for defence but mainly for the swift despatch of mortally wounded animals. One shot to the head is normally sufficient. I do not hold with animals suffering.'

I heard Cindy Applebloom exhale. She opened her eyes wide and stared at Jolyon Downside, who smiled a gentle smile.

'Now, this weapon,' continued Hiram Sidewinder, 'is not for long-distance use. No good at all for further than ten metres. Hell, those John Wayne movies have caused nothing but trouble, handguns spraying bullets all over the place. So this is for use only if they breach the first line of defence.'

It was Edouard's turn to close his eyes and adopt an expression of deep pain.

'If they breach the first line of defence it can be used at short range. It would be the last ditch before . . .'

'Excuse me,' said Cindy Applebloom, 'I must just go somewhere.' She rose and left the table, accompanied by Jolyon Downside.

'Hell,' said Hiram Sidewinder, 'did I say something to upset the lady?'

'Yes,' I said quietly, 'yes, Hiram, I think you did. I think we should try to look on the positive side.'

'Okay, okay, I take your point. Ah, Jolyon, I see you're back. Is the lady all right?'

'She's in the lavatory,' said Jolyon Downside. 'I expect she will be back shortly.'

'Well, Jolyon, I suggest we give the gun to you.'

'But I have no licence.'

'Hell, no licence, out here in the bush, in an emergency?'

'And I don't know how to shoot a pistol.'

'I thought you said you learnt about firearms at your school? In the Cadet Force. I like the idea of this Cadet Force, that's very, very good. That's what should happen to all kids, they should learn to handle automatic, semi-automatic weapons, assault rifles, all of that. But they didn't teach you to use a handgun?'

'No, I'm afraid not, I've never touched one.'

'Didn't you say you were in that movie, playing a German officer?'

'Yes, I was, and there was a handgun which was part of the uniform but I don't think I ever took it out of its holster. Don't even know if it was real. It was a very small part. I just said "*Ach so, mein Führer*" and then got blown up, lost a leg. That was it really.'

'Well, I think I can show you. Shooting a handgun is not that difficult at close range. Don't try and hit anything more than five metres away. When we finish here I'll just give you a little lesson.'

At this point, Cindy Applebloom returned to the dining table. She had about her an air of suffering and her complexion was very pale.

'Hi Cindy,' said Hiram Sidewinder, 'great to have you back. I was going to give the gun, the handgun, to Jolyon here to use only as a last resort. No more than five metres. If there is no time for a head shot then this Smith and Wesson packs one hell of a punch even to a charging ape. Two charging apes, more difficult—'

'I think I must go again,' said Cindy Applebloom and disappeared.

'Hell,' said Hiram Sidewinder, 'she's obviously not well.'

'I'll go and see what I can do,' said Winnie Sidewinder.

Hiram Sidewinder smiled at Jolyon Downside. 'I think we all understand, Jolyon, we all understand women's problems and all that but she'll feel better soon and it will be good to hear that you are armed and ready to defend her.'

'Could we get on?' said Jolyon Downside.

'Right, I've been giving this thought and I want to set out where the guns should be. So we now have four guns and Jolyon here with the revolver. We need two guns up on the balcony facing the forest, so that will be Randy, who is up there already, and Violet with her little gun.' He smiled at Violet, who solemnly nodded. 'Then we come to downstairs. Our main firepower should be aimed towards the forest. Winnie and I will occupy this role. We will be on the open area behind the dining table, which we will now overturn as a form of barricade. Josh will take the open end by the bar and will cover the ground between us and the cottages.'

'What should we do?' said Edouard quietly, from the end of the table.

'Those not immediately engaged in combat will be in a support role. Their job will be to bring water and sustenance to those in the front line.'

Beside me Claire leaned forward and placed her head in her hands.

'Is that okay? Are we all agreed? Good, good. Now I've been thinking about these rules of engagement. There is a problem here. If, and only if, there was to be a sudden charge of, say, a hundred apes emerging from the forest we would have barely sixty metres before they would be upon us. You tell us, Arthur, that they can be on that balcony in two seconds. Given the time needed to cross sand, that allows us barely ten seconds before we are overwhelmed. So there is only one way we can deal with this. *Pre-emptive strike* as we see them leave the forest. We must drop a few right there and then. The effect will be dramatic. Nothing holds up an advance like seeing your comrades fall. So, in that eventuality, I suggest it is myself who should take the responsibility for giving the order for a pre-emptive strike. If that does not work then it must be fire at will.'

Edouard was on his feet. 'I will not have the chimpanzees killed from this lodge by way of a pre-emptive strike. I say again, I insist that no firearms be used without reference to me.'

'I am sorry, Edouard,' said Hiram Sidewinder, 'I am really very sorry but I have been giving this a lot of thought. This is the only way, the only way. We may be out of here early in the morning and, my God, I hope we are, but it is in the early morning that animals do their killing. That's when they come out and kill. I know about animal behaviour. I haven't killed all the animals I have killed without knowing something about animal behaviour. It is in the early morning that they are most dangerous. I can remember being charged by a hippo at six o'clock in the morning. I was between him and the water, you see. That was a mistake but it was the time of the morning that mattered. He needed to be in that water and he came straight at me. I got him in the nose. That was lucky. When they examined

107

the body they found I'd hit him straight in the nostril, a damn difficult shot. But, here, we are not going to be that lucky. There may be a hundred apes out there and I'm not going to take any risks. I'm sorry, Edouard, but my entire family is here. No, Edouard, you may insist as much as you like but I am afraid that I must take control. Now I suggest we take our positions for the night. This Dump is not going to win while Hiram Sidewinder is alive.'

CHAPTER 15

I sat at the bar with a large glass of red wine from the Boschendal vineyard in South Africa. It tasted soft, plummy and normal. The canvas walls facing the sea had been secured and zipped but I could see along the beach past the silhouette of Josh Sidewinder, his rifle resting on the back of a chair set before him. The wind had dropped, apart from the odd gust which rustled the thatch above my head and the fringes of the jungle. A nearly new moon illuminated the white sand, now only occasionally obscured by cloud. Like the wine it felt reassuring and normal. We would be able to embark on the boat at first light. I looked at my watch. It was a little after two, barely four and a half hours to go. I heard a footstep behind me and turned, expecting Claire. Instead I was confronted by Winnie Sidewinder.

'I wonder,' she said, 'if I can have a quick word with you, Arthur?'

'Of course,' I replied. 'Can I get you a drink?'

'Sure, that would be kind. Gin, please, and a little tonic.'

While I poured her drink on the far side of the bar she called to her son, five metres away. 'All right, Josh?'

'I sure am,' said Josh Sidewinder, 'all nice and peaceful.'

I passed her glass across the bar and remained facing her. 'Is that enough tonic?'

She tasted the mix and nodded her approval. 'That's just fine and dandy.'

After a pause she continued, 'Arthur, I want to talk about my husband, about Hiram. No, no, I think we need to clear the air. I get the feeling that you don't exactly like my husband, or don't approve of him, anyway?'

'Mrs Sidewinder, Winnie, I hardly know him at all. It seems we have been here a long time but it has been barely a day.'

'Sure, sure, but first impressions are important, Arthur, and I will be blunt. You think my husband is a redneck son-of-a-bitch from the deep South. You think he's a trigger-happy, infantile cowboy slaughtering the world's wild animals.'

I took a long sip of my wine. 'Well, it is true, I don't like shooting wild animals, especially if it is done for pleasure and, in particular, if they are endangered as a species.'

'Well, you are, of course, entitled to your view but I want you to know that he was very upset about that giraffe.'

'I'm sure he was.'

'No, it made him look so bad. Have you seen the size of a giraffe? They are enormous and he was barely thirty metres away. If he had intended to kill it, it would have been like shooting at a barn door. It really upset him. He wasn't aiming at the goddamn giraffe. I know, I was there.'

'It is unfortunate then that there is a photograph of him with his foot on the neck of the animal.'

'Sure, he was persuaded to do that, and if you look at the photograph closely, he doesn't look happy, he doesn't look happy at all. In fact, he looks downright morose.'

'Mrs Sidewinder, Winnie, I don't think this is a . . .'

'No, no. Let's set aside the hunting. We are in this predicament together and it is important that we know each other. I want you to know that my husband is a very fine dentist.'

'I'm sure he is.'

'No, he is the best dentist in the whole of Tennessee. He has the kindest, gentlest manner. They don't like going to the dentist, Arthur, they don't like it at all, but all the patients say that with my husband the experience is a pleasure, a pleasure. Sure, he's expensive. Not that expensive, mind you, eight hundred dollars for an extraction, now that's pretty reasonable in Memphis, and two thousand five hundred dollars for an implant is pretty goddamn reasonable.'

'I'm sure it is.'

'No, no, here's another thing I want you to know. He has a deeply charitable side which most people don't know and don't see. Why, once a year, for a whole day, he opens his surgery free to the little black kids in Georgetown. That's the black area in Memphis and it is huge. You know, Arthur, people think coloured kids have got good teeth. They think they have got good teeth because the teeth are white and they shine out from their little black faces and so because of that *juxtaposition* people think those little black kids with their smiley faces got real good teeth. But that is not true, Arthur, that is not true. Those black kids got exactly the same tooth problem as the white kids, worse because they got such a deplorable diet.' She paused, drank deeply from her gin and uttered a small laugh. 'Not that they eat yams and black-eyed peas any more, Arthur, although that was, itself, a pretty healthy diet. No, they eat beefburgers and drink fizzy drinks. Do you know how much sugar there is in a can of Yum-Yum Light? No, you don't. There's the equivalent of an entire cupful of sugar in Yum-Yum Light, and so, whatever

111

they may look like, they've got terrible teeth. And so, once year, all day, Hiram Sidewinder, the best dentist in Memphis, Tennessee, works all day, for free, a-filling and a-pulling, all day. It is not only his own time, he pays personally for his assistants, two of them, and also for the receptionist, who, incidentally, is coloured. She got a degree in psychology which, frankly, is pretty goddamn useless in Tennessee. But she's a good girl and a damn good receptionist. I just wanted you to know this, Arthur, so you don't judge my husband too harshly. He's a good man and a damn good father to Randy, Josh and Violet. Don't judge him too harshly.'

'Mrs Sidewinder, Winnie, I don't judge your husband at all.'

'I don't think that's right. I've been watching you and your good wife. Sometimes when he is speaking you look quite pained and I know he can appear a little rough sometimes but he's the gentlest, kindest man and he wouldn't let an animal suffer. Hell, I've seen him go after a lion that he's shot in the backside all day in the African sun in order to put it out of its misery. He followed that lion for damn near four miles. When he got there, it was dead but if it hadn't been dead he would have killed it. He's still got that lion's head on his surgery wall.' Winnie Sidewinder finished her gin in a single gulp. 'Well, it's been nice talking to you, Arthur. We are not going to see much of each other now. We should be on that boat in about four hours and then we will go our separate ways but I want you to know, finally, that if there is a confrontation, that if there is a war against those apes, that he is the best man, the best man to have on your side.'

'I don't doubt it, Winnie. Would you like another gin?'

'Hell, no, I've got to get back to my post. Hiram and I said we would take it turns to have a little nap. I know you say those apes don't hunt at night, Arthur, and you know better than anyone, but Hiram Sidewinder don't take no chances. That's the kind of man he is.'

Winnie Sidewinder left the bar and returned to the dining area, now heavily fortified with furniture on the beach side. 'To the barricades,' she said as she left, 'to the barricades.'

CHAPTER 16

I finished my wine and contemplated one of the two sofas that Claire and I had drawn up for the night. I knew that she was in the library above and so I mounted the stairs in order to find her. She was in one of the deep library chairs, fast asleep. She had been reading a copy of Jane Goodall's *Innocent Killers*, her first and most famous study of chimpanzees. Beyond her, on two sofas pulled together, Jolyon Downside and Cindy Applebloom could be seen under the covers brought from their hut. I looked at Claire, who was sleeping peacefully, and reflected that there was little point in waking her for the three and a half hours that still remained until dawn. I gently removed the book, descended the stairs and resumed my position at the bar. Sleep, for me, was out of the question. I poured myself another large glass of red wine and applied myself to the first chapter of *Innocent Killers*, which I knew practically by heart. I then heard footsteps on the stairs and was surprised to see Cindy Applebloom arrive at the dining area and cross into the bar.

'Hello,' she said. 'I wonder if I could talk to you?'

I smiled. 'Of course, it's a regular service. Would you like a drink? Gin, tonic?'

She nodded vigorously and sat down on one of the bar stools recently vacated by Winnie Sidewinder. She watched in silence while I mixed her drink and pushed it across the bar.

'Cheers,' I said.

In the light of the small solar lamp on the bar I examined her closely. She had a beautiful face but now it was drawn with anxiety. She appeared to have aged.

'Well,' I said, affecting a cheerful tone, 'what can I do for you? I haven't got long. In three hours we will be leaving for the boat.' Neither the tone or the message appeared to impress her. As Winnie Sidewinder had done barely thirty minutes before, she took a long gulp of her gin and set down her glass on the surface of the bar.

'I have to tell you,' she said, 'that I am very frightened and I want to ask your advice.'

'Of course,' I said, abandoning my previous levity, 'of course. Why are you frightened?'

'I know you think it won't happen. I know your views on the chimpanzees and you are one of the world's experts, but things have happened here which you accept are not normal.'

I nodded slowly before she continued. 'First there was the Bellingham sisters. I think about them all the time. And then there was the Chinese gentleman, I've forgotten his name.'

'Yojo,' I said.

'Yes, yes, that's right. Remember, I was the one who moved the head. I shouldn't have done it but I was a nurse, you see, before I went on the stage. I shouldn't have done that, gone on the stage I mean, but I met this film producer when he was in my hospital with gallstones. The film producer, that is. He said that I was very beautiful and persuaded me to have a screen test, which I passed. It was foolish really. I know I am not a very good actor. I was a much better nurse.'

I was not expected to comment so I alternately shook and nodded my head.

'And then when I saw him under the bed or, at least, I thought he was under the bed, I reacted as a nurse. You know what happened. You saw it. When I pulled it, it just came off, or, rather, it didn't come off as there was nothing else there. It was a terrible shock and I haven't felt well ever since.'

She paused and I said: 'But Miss Applebloom, Cindy, that is entirely natural.'

'No, no, I should have been better. I should have been more professional, but there is no training for it, you understand, suddenly having a head in your hands like that. And the spectacles, just looking up at me. I see them every time I close my eyes.'

She had finished her gin and, without enquiry, I poured another. 'Thank you,' she said, 'I really shouldn't drink all this but it does make me feel better.' She drank a large gulp and replaced her glass on the bar. Instinctively I covered her hand with mine.

'You have had the most distressing, most distressing experience but, just think, in barely three hours you will be on the boat, we will be sailing across the lake and all this will be over.'

'I know. I keep on trying to think that and it is a great comfort. Is there any chance of us going earlier?'

'No, I am afraid not. The lake is treacherous at night, even in good weather. This storm has nearly passed but it will still be rough and difficult out in the centre of the lake. Far better to wait for first light and then we will all be off together.'

She looked straight at me, her eyes wide with fear and

trepidation. 'You see, I know you think it isn't going to happen, I know you do and you are, after all, our best expert, but I can't help it, I have to ask you, if, in the next three hours, there is a . . .' She hesitated before saying, 'An invasion of apes. If this Ronald Dump that you mention has, indeed, infected them, made them not *normal*, if they attack us and we are overrun,' she took another large glug of her gin, 'if we are overrun, what will happen to the women?'

'I'm sorry?'

'There are three of us here, Winnie Sidewinder and me and little Violet. I know she's got a gun but she is, after all, a mere child. What will happen to us if you, the men, are all . . . dead?' She removed her hand from under mine in order to brush away a tear. 'What will they do to us?'

'You mean,' I said gently, 'will you be in any way molested?'

'Or worse.'

'Yes, I understand what you are saying but it will not happen. There will not be an invasion of chimpanzees. It is just inconceivable. Look,' I said, holding Jane Goodall's book, 'this is the greatest single book on chimpanzees. This lady who wrote it is the world's foremost expert on chimpanzees. She knows them better than anyone else on earth and far better than me. She became very close to the chimpanzees, very close indeed. There has never been, ever, any suggestion that chimpanzees have the slightest interest in women or, indeed, any humans in that way.'

As I watched her, I saw her face relax and I continued. 'They would not find you remotely attractive, any more than you find them appealing, and you certainly don't find them attractive, do you?'

She swallowed hard. 'No, I don't, not at all but I can't get it out of my head. I keep on thinking of all that hair, all that fur and, I am sorry to say, those enormous . . .'

'Yes, yes, I know but please don't distress yourself. Treat it as a dream, a nightmare, that is all, and now you are awake and very soon it will be dawn. We will be on a boat ride and this will be just like a terrible dream. There, do you feel better?' She brushed away another tear and nodded.

'Another gin?' She nodded and I fetched the bottle which I noticed was nearly empty. 'There you are,' I said, tipping the remains into her glass. 'Just a little tonic?' She watched me as I pushed the glass towards her.

'Thank you,' she said, 'I do feel a lot better. It is just that I kept on looking at the revolver. You know, the one that Hiram gave to Jolyon. I kept on thinking, would I, could I, should I . . .' She lifted her right hand, extended two fingers to imitate a gun and placed them at the side of her head. 'You know, bang.'

I decided on stern common sense and said: 'Cindy, please do not talk like that. Do not even consider it.'

She drank half of her gin in a single swallow. 'I know, I know I am being foolish but I keep thinking of the Bellingham sisters. Out there they didn't have a revolver. They were defenceless.'

'I know, and that is very serious, but when we get back we will make a full report. Tanzanian Park Rangers will be deployed and there will be a thorough search. Helicopters will be used. We will find the Bellingham sisters. Have no fear.'

She nodded again. 'Thank you, thank you so much. I feel a lot better now. I suspect it is the gin but you have cheered me up.' She raised her right hand again to her temple. 'No bang then?'

'Certainly not, no bang. Now I suggest you take that back upstairs. Jolyon will be wondering where you have gone.'

'Yes, I think you are right. Only two and a half hours to go.'

'Two and a half hours,' I said. She was a little unsteady when she left the bar but paused at the foot of the stairs and smiled towards me. 'No bang.'

'No bang,' I said.

I heard her footsteps on the floor above and immediately afterwards saw Claire at the head of the stairs. She descended to the dining area and came over to the bar. 'No bang?' she said, raising an eyebrow. 'What was all that about?'

'Pre-emptive suicide,' I said, 'nothing serious. It was all to avoid rape by ape.'

'Yes, all that hair. Don't fancy it myself. Any chance you can find me a drink?'

'I think I can manage. You're my third customer in about an hour. Very popular, this bar.'

'Not surprising, classy barman. A large gin please.'

'You're out of luck, darling. I have just emptied the bottle for my last customer. Wine, whisky? I think there is some vodka somewhere.'

'Large vodka and tonic and look sharpish. What about him?' She nodded in the direction of Josh Sidewinder.

I called down the bar. 'Josh, you want a drink? Have a beer?'

He turned and called back: 'No thanks, it would send me to sleep. Could do with a Coke though.'

As Claire took him the can I poured a large vodka and tonic and helped myself to another glass of wine, which finished the bottle. I was beginning to feel slightly drunk and resolved to take it slowly.

'You've got my book,' Claire said, turning to the bar stool recently occupied by Winnie Sidewinder and Cindy Applebloom. 'I wondered where it had gone.'

'Yes, I took it. It had obviously sent you to sleep.'

'It always does. Primate research, even by the best, is a great soporific.'

She sipped her drink and sat staring at the photograph of Jane Goodall on the back of the book. 'She won't like it, will she? She won't like our report, what happened here, the Bellinghams and the Chinaman with no head, or rather no body and all head.'

'No, she won't like it; she probably won't believe it. She never did like this lodge very much – commercial undertaking, exploiting her chimpanzees.'

'They are not her chimpanzees, they are our chimpanzees, and I always thought her aversion to this place was unreasonable. Certainly Edouard has made some money. He's made a profit from the likes of the Sidewinders and the Downsides but it's a *learned*, liberal, well-earned profit. We all obeyed the rules here. We were on their side. We wore the masks to stop diseases and we kept our distance. We obeyed the rules.'

'I didn't,' I said, drinking my wine.

'What do you mean, you didn't? You were always a scrupulous researcher.'

'I didn't with Dump.'

She looked at me and shook her head. 'You didn't have any choice. He was going to kill Ajax, who was hiding behind you for protection. You had a panga. You were lucky that you got him. He would have killed you too.'

'Chimps don't kill humans.'

'This one does.' She was suddenly serious. 'This one has killed three at least. Where does that fit in with your *Innocent Killers, Visions of Caliban, Brutal Kinship*? Where do you find the psychopathic ape? How does Ronald Dump fit into all that scholarship? Still less *The Prototype Primate*.'

'There is no proof yet.'

'No, there is no proof. But we are all the same, researchers, academics or, as Winnie Sidewinder says, wet liberals. We study them and write about them, like them, even grow to love them, and all the while their world is being destroyed. Their homeland is being scorched and torched, their forests are going to the industrial machine of the Chinese Empire. What do we do to stop it? Nothing.' She stopped, shook her head. 'But I'm getting maudlin. It's that time of night. All the spooks come out. What time is it anyway?'

'Nearly five. I think I can see dawn over the mountains. In an hour we can start packing up some food, have some breakfast, then beat a retreat to the boat, surrounded by firearms, and leave.'

She dismounted from the stool and walked towards the stairs. 'I'm going to assemble all of Jane's books and the other volumes. It is the best research library in Africa and we need to take it with us.'

'You think we are not coming back?'

She turned at the foot of the stairs. 'No one is coming back after what has happened here. No one will come back. Just Chinese loggers. Have you got his specs, by the way? If I were you I'd leave them on the bar. That will confuse the coppers.'

As she mounted the stairs I heard her walking softly backwards and forwards on the library floor above me. Periodically there was a soft thud which I assumed to be the collected works of Jane Goodall, Richard Wrangham, Dian Fossey and Hugo van Lawick hitting the floor. Well, it would keep her occupied. The lake was now invisible behind the canvas sheeting but I could tell from the noise of the waves that it was calm enough for our voyage. The dawn unfolded slowly over the mountains. It was going to be a fine, calm, gentle day.

CHAPTER 17

I finished my wine and sat on one of the sofas. I must have slept a little. When I woke Edouard was standing above me, gently shaking my shoulder. 'Come,' he said, 'it is nearly six o'clock, it is nearly dawn.' I looked at the entrance to the bar and beyond to the white beach and the forest, now clearly visible in the morning light. Josh Sidewinder was standing at the entrance, surveying the beach through the telescopic sight of his rifle.

'Please wake the others if they are asleep. I will go down to the boat and see that it is ready.'

'I'll go with you,' said Josh Sidewinder.

'There is no need.'

'Why, hell, there is. You need an armed escort. I know it is only a matter of forty metres but, all the same, we shouldn't take chances.'

Edouard shrugged, then nodded and they both left through the bar.

Their progress across the sand was blocked from view by the canvas sheets which still covered the lake side of the lodge. I climbed the stairs to the library. Jolyon Downside and Cindy Applebloom were already up and dressed. Claire was standing contemplating a large pile of books.

'Do you think we could take all those?' she said.

'I don't know. I'll ask Edouard when he gets back.'

Violet Sidewinder appeared from behind an armchair as Randy Sidewinder came in from the balcony. I crossed to the opposite side of the library and unzipped one of the canvas panels. From the open balcony it was possible to see the beach and the jetty beyond. There was no sign of Edouard or Josh Sidewinder. And there was no boat. Possibilities crowded into my brain. They had taken it out for a test? To refuel? To pick up further supplies? None of them made any sense. I crossed to the opposite balcony, from where I could see the forest which surrounded the kitchen and the staff area. There was movement in the trees and, briefly, I saw black figures swinging through the high branches. I gripped the balustrade with both hands.

'Edouard,' I shouted, 'Edouard, where are you?' There was no reply. I called again, louder, 'Edouard, Edouard, where is the boat?' I was now joined by Claire and Violet and Randy Sidewinder. Below me, in the entrance to the lodge, I saw Hiram Sidewinder emerge from behind the barricade of furniture. Winnie Sidewinder joined him. There was further movement in the lower branches by the edge of the sand and I swore softly with relief when two figures, Edouard and Josh, emerged from the kitchen path. They ran towards the lodge and then disappeared below me. I saw both of them from the stairs as I went down into the dining area, with the remaining members of the group following me.

Edouard turned to me, his face moving in a mixture of anger and resignation.

'They have gone,' he said. 'They have taken the bloody boat.'

'Who?' I asked.

'The staff, all of them. They have all disappeared. They must have taken the boat. It is gone, there is no sign of it.'

'When, do you think?'

'God knows, early I suspect. We did not see or hear them because of the bloody canvas. They could have gone any time before five. The kitchen is open and empty. There is food. They have left food for us on the table in the kitchen. No message.'

Behind me on the stairs I heard a cry. Cindy Applebloom was clutching Jolyon Downside. 'Oh my God,' she cried, 'oh my God, we're trapped.'

I turned to Edouard. 'The radio?'

'I have tried the radio. Benedict and Boniface both have radios. Neither is answering. Either they are far out into the lake or else the radios are turned off. It doesn't really matter which.'

John Boxe had emerged unnoticed from the service area of the dining room. 'I still can't get a signal,' he said, 'on the satellite phone.'

Edouard shook his head with irritation. 'I have already put out a Mayday signal on the radio. I have asked for any alternative boat and also requested the helicopter. Unhappily it appears that it is being serviced but I have requested it nonetheless. We must assume that it is their intention, the intention of the staff, to return the boat as soon as they have reached Akawi. Assuming that they left at five a.m., they will be back by eleven. That is barely four and a half hours from now. I suggest that we make preparations to leave immediately and, for the moment, we will maintain all the security arrangements. Josh has brought some food with him from the kitchen. It is only bread rolls, I am afraid, with some jam and marmalade. We are able to make tea and coffee here and so I suggest that we breakfast as best we can. I am confident that headquarters will have received our radio communications and that everything will be done to ensure our evacuation.'

'Hell,' said Hiram Sidewinder, 'well, if we have to keep our defensive positions for a few hours then that's okay. Boys, why don't you get some coffee going with your mother? This is the kind of setback which leads to improved morale and team work. Let's all co-operate and pull together.'

He had barely finished his sentence when the bells started to ring from the vacated huts. Within a minute all eight huts' bells had been activated and continued to ring.

'Christ,' said Randy, 'they're in all of the huts. They're calling for room service.'

'There ain't no staff,' said Josh.

'The staff's all gone on the boat,' said Violet.

'Hell,' said Hiram Sidewinder, 'they don't want room service, they just want to torment us. "Come out here," they are saying, "come out here, like your Chinaman."'

Minutes passed and the bells slowly died away. They were replaced with a noise which grew in the jungle. The sounds were the same, the eerie long cry of the hunting chimpanzee. Gradually they grew in unison until the whole forest and mountainside vibrated with the noise. Then, suddenly, it changed. The call continued but it was overlaid with another repeated sound like a massive and simultaneous exhalation of breath, 'Humph!'

Hiram Sidewinder took hold of his gun, walked to the barricade and stared into the jungle.

'That's the only thing to do, a warning salvo.'

Josh and Randy Sidewinder joined their father, side by side, guns at the ready, before Edouard shouted: 'Stop! You cannot fire above their heads. You are firing into the mountainside. They could be anywhere out there, in any of the trees.'

Hiram Sidewinder scanned the jungle for signs of movement. There was none.

'That goddamn noise, it just gets on your nerves. *Humph, humph, humph*. It must mean something. What are they saying? What are they doing?' He turned to me. 'Arthur, you are the expert. You know these chimpanzees better than anyone else. What does it mean? What are they saying?'

I shrugged and shook my head. 'I don't know; I just don't know. I have never heard it before. Nor have I read about it.'

'One thing's for sure,' said Hiram Sidewinder, turning back to the jungle, 'this ain't friendly, this is not friendly, so what do we do? Four hours 'til the boat gets back, what do we do? Just stay at our posts and wait?'

Edouard said: 'Yes, that is all we can do and, above all, we must not panic. May I emphasise we should not take any offensive action. We must not make it any worse.'

We resumed the positions we had taken the night before. Hiram and Winnie Sidewinder stood behind the barricade at the jungle side of the lodge. John Boxe continued to take photographs. Josh Sidewinder took up a position at the entrance to the bar from which he could see all the guest huts along the fringes of the jungle. Periodically a bell sounded, indicating that one or the other was occupied. Of the occupants themselves, there was no sign. Jolyon Downside and Cindy Applebloom elected to stay downstairs in the bar. Claire and I climbed the stairs to the library. Here Violet and Randy Sidewinder were on the balcony facing the jungle. Their guns rested against the balustrade. I looked at the pile of texts that Claire had placed on the floor. There were obviously too many to take; perhaps a hundred books in different languages.

I noticed that she had placed *The Prototype Primate* on top of the pile, a substantial volume, quarto size and three inches thick. I picked it up, turned to the third page, which contained acknowledgements, and read aloud: 'I am deeply grateful to Claire Watkins, without whose help and advice this book could not have been written.'

'Liar,' said Claire. 'Sexual stimulus more like.'

I smiled, turned the page and silently read the manuscript dedication. 'For Edouard Deprès, the Serole Lodge and the Serole family, one of the last outposts of civilisation. May 2009.'

Claire was reading it over my shoulder. 'Pretentious bugger,' she said.

I replaced the book and noticed with a little alarm that my hand was shaking.

'We can't take them all. We should sort them out. Edouard will help us.'

'I agree,' said Claire. 'You go and find him and I'll divide them up.'

I descended the stairs again and found Edouard by the bar entrance, talking to Jolyon Downside. He had his back to the beach and did not see the sudden movement that was apparent to Downside and myself. From close to the furthest hut three figures had emerged and were running along the sand. Shortly they were followed by a fourth, slower than the first three and losing ground.

'My God,' said Downside, 'here they come, here they come.'

I had recognised them the moment I saw them and so had Edouard. As they grew closer, within one hundred metres, I heard Edouard shout: 'Ajax, Horatio and Brutus and I think that's Gertrude behind, yes, it is.'

128

The chimpanzees were moving at full speed across the beach. Chimpanzees do not like sand. Their hands and feet, made for climbing and gripping trees, do not suit a soft and yielding surface. Normally they would have kept to the fringe of the jungle and the trees. I saw Josh Sidewinder slip the safety catch on his rifle and heard the unmistakable click as his father operated the bolt action on his weapon. Edouard and I shouted at the same time: 'No, no, do not shoot, no one must shoot.'

I continued to shout as I ran back into the dining area. 'These are friends, these are friends. Don't shoot.' I moved out beyond the barricade and watched as they approached. I waved my hands in a futile gesture of welcome and still had them above my head when a shot rang out from the balcony. Along the beach I saw Gertrude stop suddenly and fall to her side. From the balcony I heard Violet Sidewinder shout: 'Daddy, I got one! I've got me an ape!'

Behind me I heard a roar of anger and Edouard sprinted up the stairs. As I followed I heard him shout, 'You imbecile, you imbecile. What are you doing? You imbecile. You have shot our friend! Our friend. You were told not to shoot.'

'I was given the order to shoot.'

'No, you were told not to shoot. You imbecile, you little fool. You are a killer, a bloody, bloody fool!'

'They are coming in,' shouted Hiram Sidewinder below me.

Ajax, Horatio and Brutus had reached the flimsy furniture barricade, which they all cleared in one leap. Below me I heard Cindy Applebloom scream. Edouard and I leapt down the stairs. In the dining area we found the three chimpanzees, their backs to the canvas wall, all emitting sounds of distress. '*Kuk, kuk, kuk.*'

'Ajax, Ajax, it's me,' I cried.

All three had obviously been fighting. Ajax had an ugly wound across his chest. Horatio stared at me from one eye, the other a mass of blood. Brutus appeared unharmed except that one arm hung motionless by his side. He repeatedly pulled it with the other, causing it to swing in its socket. As he did so he exhaled breath, the primate's scream of pain. Edouard moved slowly towards them and then squatted on his haunches, both arms extended. The noises of distress gradually subsided. From behind me I heard Hiram Sidewinder say, 'What the hell, what the hell, who are these guys? Who are these guys?' I turned to confront him, fighting the anger within me. 'These are Serole chimps, they come from the Serole family. They may be all that remain. Certainly after that.' I pointed through the open bar area on to the beach. Forty metres away, Gertrude lay on her side. 'He,' I said, pointing to Ajax behind me, is the alpha male of the group and she,' I said, pointing across the beach, 'is the oldest female. Or was the oldest female.'

Hiram Sidewinder followed my pointing finger and then shouted, 'My God, my God, it is still alive.' As we watched, Gertrude rolled over and attempted to rise. She succeeded in getting on to all fours before she collapsed back on to the sand.

CHAPTER 18

Extracts from Serole Research Log

21 October 2005
Ajax has become solitary. He spends time with Gertrude most days. Then he passes among the troupe and occasionally plays with the young chimps. He seldom hunts and for long periods he is alone. In the weeks after the punishment of Ronald he kept close to Regan while she rapidly recovered. She is now pregnant. Ronald disappeared into the jungle for days. When he reappeared he seemed a reformed character. He hangs around Hector and the other dominant males, adopting a submissive posture whenever Ajax approaches. He pointedly ignores his mother, who also ignores him.

29 October 2005
Ajax has taken to sitting on my veranda. Normally he occupies the steps but occasionally climbs onto the swinging day bed suspended from the rafters. Sometimes he is joined by Gertrude or Darwin, a small effeminate male who grooms his leader's fur while chattering quietly into his ear. When I go into the forest to deal with field work I often leave him sitting like a sentry outside my door. When I return he acknowledges me by shaking his large head. I feel strangely privileged.

5 November 2005

I have started talking to Ajax. When I do so he shifts his attention from the lake or the jungle and watches me with apparent comprehension. He does not respond but occasionally strokes his chin. It invites confidences and today I unburdened myself of a secret. 'It's about Claire Watkins, my research colleague,' I said. 'You may have noticed that we have become quite close, very close in fact. I think you know that she often spends the night with me here, more often than not. I know the business takes rather longer than yours but we enjoy it just the same.'

I paused and watched him but his black eyes did not move. He appeared to be concentrating. I persevered. 'She has been away for the last two weeks. She has gone across the lake to Rwanda. When she comes back I want to ask her to marry me. I am worried that she will refuse. If she does it may ruin our relationship here, now, which is pretty wonderful. What do you think? You're the boss, the chief, the law giver. What do you think?'

Did he understand the interrogative pause? He continued to watch me, the great black eyes unblinking. Then he stroked his chin and with one movement swung to the ground and made off into the jungle. As I watched he gave what I believed to be a barely perceptible shrug. I am a scientist. Studying chimpanzees demands the ruthless rejection of anthropomorphic interpretation. But I am also a man in love. Did I see him shrug? Does it matter? It said it all. 'Don't be a gibbering idiot. Ask her.'

24 May 2006

The reformation of Ronald has come to an end. In the last six months he has grown enormously. Standing upright he is now a head taller than Hector and bigger than Ajax. He has reverted to bullying and haphazard delinquency. Yesterday I heard a commotion in the fig trees that stand fifty metres behind the lodge, followed by the piercing scream of a chimpanzee in sudden pain and fear. I made what speed I could through the forest (you never run) and met Darwin bounding towards me. He was moving on three legs and whimpering. When he saw me he stopped briefly before plunging into thick bush. I had time to see his right hand. On two fingers the nails were missing and blood was pulsing through the fur. When I turned back to the trees I was confronted by Ronald. He reared up and curled his upper lip away from his teeth. On them fresh blood could clearly be seen. It was followed by a familiar routine. He turned, squatted and vented his bowels as I backed away.

This morning a new problem emerged. The lodge is half full and the guests include a family from Barking in Essex. The husband and father, Graham Burton, is apparently engaged in the sale of mortgages on a grand scale. The entire family was equipped with expensive safari clothes, hats and binoculars. Last evening they had been given Edouard's usual introduction on the subject of contact with the chimpanzees; the harmless and essentially gentle nature of the animals, the possibility of boisterous and playful behaviour and the crucial wearing of masks to prevent disease. This morning at eight thirty they set out with Moses on a half-day walk in the jungle. It finished early. I was sitting with Edouard when we were alerted by shouting from the lodge. When we arrived we found the Burton family gathered around their father. His once-immaculate safari jacket was badly soiled with excrement. He still wore the surgical mask around his neck, which also, as we watched, dripped ordure onto his footwear. Moses was standing beside him and as we arrived he silently mouthed, 'Ronald.'

'That fucking ape!' said Mr Burton, who was trying to release the buttons of his jacket with his fingers draped in a protective napkin.

Edouard attempted to introduce some calm. 'Please,' he said, 'is anyone hurt or injured?'

Mrs Burton turned on him. 'It's that fucking enormous ape. He was waiting for us at the end of the walk. Huge, he is. He did a mock charge like you said they do and Graham just made a friendly gesture, you know, eff off. Then he turns around and does his business right in front of us. The ape, that is.'

Graham Burton provided more detail. 'Did his fucking business all right, a huge bloody DUMP just feet away and then he picks it up in both hands and only chucks it straight at me. Look at my bloody jacket. If I hadn't been wearing this bloody mask it would have gone straight down my throat. And then he does this enormous grin or snarl, baring his teeth and gibbering. You didn't tell us they did that. Mock charging is one thing but dumping and chucking shit is something else.'

Edouard said, 'It has been known to happen but it is very rare.'

'Rare,' said Mrs Burton, 'I'll say it is. I suppose we will have to live with this nasty pong for the rest of the day.'

So that was it. The Burtons calmed down and even made a joke of it, connected with Basildon. They christened Ronald 'Dump', a name which is likely to stick. The staining came out of the jacket and Edouard offered a full refund, which was refused. But I am deeply uneasy. This violence and contempt is escalating. I have never seen it before and do not know where it will end.

24 May 2007
This will be my last entry. The events of yesterday were the
most extraordinary and traumatic of the whole of my period at
Serole. I am still in shock and my hand shakes as I write. The
lodge, thank God, is closed for the rainy season. There had been a
brief shower in the morning and Claire and I had spent the time
finishing our packing. Only our personal effects are left. All our
academic material has already been shipped. Edouard had given
us dinner the night before. We had drunk too much and were a
little irritable. When the rain stopped I announced that I would
take a short walk in the forest. I had not seen the Serole chimps
in nearly a week and felt bereft. This is the reason, I thought, why
I must leave before I become an ape. The rain had caused the
branches in the forest to fall and sag across the paths and I took
a panga to clear my way. I was aiming for a clearing I knew well,
surrounded by tropical oak and mahogany. The sun had begun
to shine, casting shadows beneath the trees. Distinctly, above the
steady dripping of water, I heard the distant calls of chimpanzees
emerging from shelter high in the jungle canopy.

I reached my clearing and lowered myself onto a dry log. I heard
movement in the trees and sensed I was being watched before I
saw Ajax emerge from the forest. He loped on all fours into the
centre of the open ground, sat on his haunches ten metres away
and steadily returned my gaze. I had a curious feeling that it was
an arranged meeting that I had forgotten or overlooked. I raised
the panga in salute and was about to speak when I saw the bush
spring apart behind him and a huge figure emerged. I had not
seen Dump for weeks. He was upright on two legs. In one hand he
carried a rock. Ajax heard him and half turned before he received
a terrible blow to the side of the head. He was knocked sideways,

full length on the ground, and began to rise but the rock was smashed again into the side of his face. He rolled onto his back. I could see he was barely conscious as he lifted a weak arm in front of his face. Dump circled the body, then straddled the chest and raised the rock in both hands.

At this point I cried out. It was an instinct beyond deliberation. 'Stop,' I shouted, 'stop that!' Dump paused, the rock still held above his head. He turned to look at me, then silently bared his teeth before he turned back to focus on the target below him. I had already begun to advance. Now I covered the last two metres and swung the panga. It was a wild blow aimed vaguely at the shoulder. I saw the blade bite deep into the fur and a jet of blood erupted into the air. With a loud scream he turned towards me and I saw the rock descending before I struck again and again with the panga. Never in my life had I delivered a blow in anger. Now I felt a terrible wave rise within me. I was aiming for the head and the neck, chopping back and forwards at close range. I did not feel the rock strike my head. I was possessed by a manic concentration. I felt my weapon make cut after cut and fountains of blood covered my face and eyes. Then he was gone. Through the red film I barely saw him half roll, half crawl into the bush. Only then did I realise that the roaring noise came from me, my mouth wide open, teeth fully exposed. I looked upwards at the canopy above, the weapon still clenched in my hand. And that is how they found me, motionless above Ajax whimpering and shivering at my feet.

Edouard came into my line of sight, blank horror on his face. He looked down at the fallen chimpanzee and then at the panga before I shook my head and spoke. 'Dump,' I said. He frowned then nodded. He came close and eased the panga from my grasp.

'Are you all right?' he said. I said nothing. I did not tell him I felt wonderful.

Ajax is alive. Members of the Serole troupe arrived, Gertrude, Horatio and Nixon. By that time he was able to walk and, I am told, they disappeared together into the forest. Claire took me in hand. My clothes were burnt and the blood showered from my head and arms. A little of it was mine. The rock had grazed my temple as it fell. The wound is superficial, requiring neither suture nor bandage. Moses and Benedict have tracked Dump into the jungle. It was not difficult. Vast quantities of blood covered the paths and the lower branches, indicating that he had tried unsuccessfully to swing or climb. Finally the trail disappeared into impenetrable bush. 'He is dead,' said Benedict. 'He has lost so much blood. Even if he live for a day or two he cannot hunt or eat. He will be excluded from the troupe.'

This evening at 6.30 we had a final meeting with Edouard at the lodge. He poured three large whiskies and brought them to the table with a jug of water. 'Cheers,' he said. We all drank, then he began as I knew he would. 'You have certainly finished on a memorable note, Arthur. Perhaps you would give me all the details.'

I did so. I had prepared a meticulous account. He listened with care and made not a single note. As I finished he sat for a moment, then shook his head and poured more drinks. He raised his glass. 'You broke the rules,' he said. 'You intervened.'

'If I had not done so he would have killed him.'

Edouard shrugged, 'So what? It has happened a million times before. Sometimes the alpha male gives way. Often he is killed. That is the way; if you like, the law.'

'It was a coward's attack, from behind, with a weapon.'

Edouard set down his glass and rapped the table with irritation. 'Really, Arthur, you are talking heresy. What do you expect? Your Queensberry rules, a fair fight, may the best man win, jolly good show? This is the jungle, Arthur. No one knows that better than you. This is a Hobbesian world. It can be nasty, brutish and short. These apes survive precisely because they have an alpha male. He may be cunning, devious, brutal, violent and cowardly but he means order, discipline, law. Without him there is chaos. Now you have interfered and you know you should not have done so.' He paused, then smiled. 'You are both wonderful people and you, Arthur, are a wonderful academic but you are not, repeat not a chimpanzee. You are a research fellow from Oxford, not an alpha male.'

'I don't want to be an alpha male.'

'Oh but you do. In a way we all do. It grows on you.' He was suddenly businesslike. 'So tomorrow you will leave me and I will be very sorry to see you go. But do not come back. Not for ten years at least. You may have noticed that I made no notes of your account and for me there will be no record. I cannot stop you publishing what you like but I would prefer today to be omitted entirely. No good can come of it.'

Tonight, our last at Serole, Claire and I finished a bottle of wine and went to bed. We did not sleep but after an hour she moved tight against me and kissed my lips. 'Alpha male,' she said.

CHAPTER 19

'I'm going out there,' said Hiram Sidewinder, 'I'm going out there now. The Sidewinders do not leave an animal in pain. If we have shot an animal, then we will kill it. That is my ethics. Jolyon, give me that handgun, this is my job.'

'No,' I said, 'this is *our* job. That animal is my friend. "It" is a she, and she is my friend and I am going too. If she can be saved, she is going to be saved.'

Sidewinder looked back at me. 'Arthur, I am sorry that this has happened. I truly am sorry. If I had known that she was your friend, I would have insisted that Violet did not shoot her. But you must understand that this is now a hunting matter. Judgement as to whether it . . . *she* can be saved is my judgement. Hell, I've seen animals that have taken bullets and I know whether they are going to live or die.'

I took one step towards him. He was a big man but I was taller and I saw him instinctively flinch. 'Hiram,' I said, 'I have said it once and I will say it only once more. I am coming with you and the decision as to whether she will be shot will be my decision and my decision alone.'

Heavy silence ensued, during which Jolyon Downside took the revolver from the bar and held it out between us. 'Who wants this then?'

'Give it to him,' I said. 'I will make the decision and he will pull the trigger if necessary.'

Hiram Sidewinder reasserted his authority. 'Okay, okay. Right, Randy, keep an eye on my back. You watch the edges of that jungle over there and watch my back. Winnie, are you there? Okay.'

We were about to leave when a voice behind us said, 'Can I come? This could be a wonderful opportunity.' I stared at John Boxe as he raised his camera by way of explanation. 'I've got some very good shots. I've actually got a video of the apes jumping the barrier.'

I came close to losing control. 'Mr Boxe,' I said, 'are you mad, are you stark mad?'

'No, I'm not mad, I'm a photographer. I always wanted to be a war photographer but I've got terrible asthma. It is okay at the moment and that's not very far to run. I could get a picture of you shooting the ape. No, no, okay, I'll just stay here and take photographs from the lodge.'

We left the cover of the thatch and made our way across the beach. Gertrude had not moved since her initial effort but, as we drew closer, we saw that she kept sweeping the sand with her right hand. Her left arm was bent upwards towards her head and that too could be seen moving. As we walked, apparently in time with our steps, the noise from the jungle increased, either in volume or by numbers. The same long hunting call, growing steadily in pitch and volume and then, suddenly, followed by the universal exhalation, '*Humph, humph, humph.*'

'My God,' said Hiram Sidewinder, 'my God, how many are there? How many does it take to make that noise?'

We were now closer to the fringe of the jungle and, in the higher branches, I started to see movement. Swinging shapes briefly came into view and then were lost in the canopy. We reached Gertrude's body and both knelt beside her. She was alive and conscious. Her eyes briefly opened and then closed again. Her right hand was pressed against the side of her head and I leant forward gently to pull it back. When I touched her hand her whole body jerked in spasm but she allowed me to prise her arm backwards. The bullet had passed through her throat and blood could be seen saturating the sand behind her skull. She made no attempt to move her head. Beside me Hiram Sidewinder stared down.

'I reckon she's been hit in the spine. Ain't much resistance to a bullet in the throat like that. It goes straight through and it's . . . she has lost a lot of blood.' To my amazement I saw that there were tears in his eyes. 'I ain't never seen a chimpanzee before, never. Sure I've seen monkeys and baboons, but never anything like . . . her.' He coughed slightly and I saw that a moment had passed. 'Well,' he said, 'I'm afraid she's a goner. Ain't no hope for her and it looks as if she has been wounded already.' He pointed at Gertrude's lower right leg. Just above the ankle there was a huge wound clearly visible. Bone protruded through the fur. 'That wasn't caused by a bullet,' he said, 'that's a fight all right. That's her kin done that down there. Bullet or no bullet, she wouldn't have survived that wound. I know, hell, I've seen animals . . .'

'Shut up,' I said, 'will you please shut up. As to your . . . assessment, I agree. It has to be done. You know how to do it. Please get on with it.'

Hiram Sidewinder lifted the revolver and slipped off the safety catch. He looked me straight in the eyes. 'There is one other consideration,' he said. 'If we shoot her out here, what's it going to do to the rest? There's apes in there, hundreds of them by the sounds of it. They may not like her and, by the looks of it, they have given her a really bad time but, in the end, she's one of them and we're one of us. How are they going to react to us shooting her while she's still alive?'

I stared back at him. 'You assume that they know?'

'Hell, I don't assume, I know and they'll know, they'll know all right. This Dump, this delinquent Dump, you think he's behind all of this? Well, I tell you that if it is true, he is not going to miss a trick like this. This Dump wants us dead just like the Bellinghams, just like Moses, just like that Chinaman, and he's getting 'em worked up all right, you just listen to that.' He looked at the forest, from which the noises steadily increased. 'So it may be better, from our point of view, just to say amen. I don't like it but it may be better.'

'No, she could be out here for hours like that and she's helpless. Whatever did that to her,' I pointed to the wound on her leg, 'could be capable of much worse. You shoot her, Hiram, and we will take our chance.'

'Righto, you don't have to look. There may be a lot of blood.'

I stood and looked at the jungle. It was now definitely moving right across the high canopy. Many silhouettes were now clear. Adult chimpanzees beyond doubt. Behind me I heard a single shot and then the voice of Hiram Sidewinder. 'That's all it needed, let's get going. Let's get back.'

Before he had gone ten metres he stopped and placed a hand on my arm. 'Listen,' he said. The noises in the jungle had suddenly ceased. 'The shot,' said Hiram Sidewinder, 'I told you.' Without conscious agreement, we both started to run. As we did so I saw the branches at beach level begin to move at the fringes of the jungle.

When we reached the security of the lodge the entire group gathered around us. The only absentees were Violet Sidewinder and Edouard himself.

Jolyon Downside spoke first. 'You had to kill her,' he said.

Hiram Sidewinder answered. 'Yeah, sure we did. We both agreed it was the only way.'

'But the noises, the noises have stopped,' said Downside, 'that's all stopped. It is so quiet.'

'It was the shot,' said Hiram Sidewinder, 'that's what it was, a single shot. After that there was nothing, silence.'

'My God, it's wonderful,' said Winnie Sidewinder, 'not to have to listen to that *humph, humph, humph* any more.'

'Do you think they are still there?' said Cindy Applebloom.

I looked at Claire. 'Yes, yes, they are certainly still there. Chimpanzees take time to move in family groups, but how long they will remain I can't tell. At least for the present there is no sound.'

'Well, that's a relief,' said Randy Sidewinder. 'What's the time now?'

As though on cue, Edouard appeared from the service area. He was carrying his radio. He was also smiling. 'I wonder,' he said, 'whether you would come here and gather round. I have got some good news.'

'Thank God,' said Jolyon Downside.

'The boat?' said Cindy Applebloom.

'Yes, it is the boat. I have just heard from Akawi. I have good signal strength. The weather is good, both over the mountains and across the lake.'

'And what did they say?' asked Winnie Sidewinder.

'They say that the boat has arrived, has been refuelled and is now on its way back. It will be here in a little over two hours, two and a half hours at the most. Furthermore,' he said, holding up a hand to stem the growing murmur of relief, 'furthermore, headquarters has requisitioned another boat and have requested immediate assistance from the Park Rangers on the other side of the mountain. They will fly to Akawi, pick up the boat and should be with us by the end of the day. That means that you will all be able to leave in two and a half hours. I will remain, with Arthur and Claire if they wish, and a dozen Park Rangers will be with us by nightfall. I thought you would be pleased.'

The news was greeted with a chorus of relieved sighs and some clapping. Cindy Applebloom burst into tears.

'Well, hell,' said Hiram Sidewinder, 'I think that calls for a drink. It's getting on for eight in the morning but most of us haven't had much sleep. Mine will be a large whisky. John,' he said, turning to John Boxe, 'why don't you take a photograph of us all at this moment.'

Claire and I acquiesced unwillingly to the team photograph and both of us refused liquor. The Sidewinder twins and John Boxe drank beer. Jolyon Downside and Cindy Applebloom opened a bottle of white wine.

'Violet,' cried Hiram Sidewinder, 'come down here and have a Coca-Cola. Don't you worry, it is all over. Nobody is angry with you now.'

From the library above there came no sound. I was suddenly quite exhausted. I walked to the sitting area beyond the dining room, dropped on to a sofa and closed my eyes. Hiram Sidewinder followed me.

'So, now, what's going to happen to them?' I opened my eyes and saw that he was pointing to Ajax, Horatio and Brutus, who remained crouched against the canvas wall. 'Are we going to take them with us on the boat? Is this the time for Noah's Ark? It looks as though they have had a bad time with that Dump and you think their family's gone as well? We could take them with us, release them in another park, another reserve.'

I shook my head. 'It is a nice idea but there are rules. We do not interfere in chimp behaviour, however tempting it is. We observe and research, that's all.'

'Well, I hear that,' said Hiram Sidewinder, 'but what about her?' He nodded towards a picture of Jane Goodall which hung on the wall, looking down on the dining area. It was a famous picture of Jane being embraced by two of her chimpanzees. 'What about her? That looks like interference to me.'

'That is a very early picture, but she was exceptional. She did not go to them; they came to her quite naturally. But you're right, it is controversial. For us we have a golden rule: we do not interfere.' I indicated the three chimpanzees. 'They may or may not survive. What has happened is unknown. There will be inquiries, further research. We will find out what has happened to the Serole family. They would certainly not survive if we took them to another part of the park. Chimpanzees cannot join other troupes. They are automatically rejected. And then there is the logging.'

'The logging, yeah, Christ, I heard about that. That's really bad, really bad. The destruction of their habitat, their homes. Chinese interests, aren't they? Chinese?'

'They are, yes.'

'The Chinese are a goddamn menace to the chimpanzees and they are a goddamn menace to us. The Chinese and the Muslims, they are the root of all our problems, the Chinese and the Muslims. Some people say it's the Mexicans but I say

Chinese and Muslims.' He was silent for a moment, drinking from his whisky glass. 'That's what I do, you see, I interfere. I kill animals. I know you don't agree with that but I do. But it keeps their habitat. These Africans, they are goddamn corrupt, I know that. You've got to pay 'em to keep the habitat for the animals to live in. What's more, I hear that you did interfere. I hear you interfered to fight off this Dump, that you fought him off with a panga. That you thought you'd killed him, that's what started all this, this Dump. He's an aberrant delinquent, right? He's mad, psychologically unbalanced. If he was human, we would lock him up or stick him in an electric chair or gas him or something. If you hadn't interfered he would have killed that chimp over there and become the alpha male and you would have him where you could see him. Yeah, you could control him, but instead of that he went wild and now he's out there, or rather it appears that he's not out there any more. Thank God.'

I was exhausted and, to tell the truth, a little bored. 'Hiram,' I said, 'if you don't mind, I am very tired. I was up all night. I'd like to argue with you but I haven't got the energy.'

'Sure, sure, fine by me but I think I'll just get myself another drink. Do you want one?'

I shook my head and smiled what I hoped was a weary smile, leaned backwards and closed my eyes. At that precise moment the gentle hum of conversation was silenced by a deafening crash and the splintering of wood. This was immediately followed by a scream from the landing above.

'Violet,' cried Winnie Sidewinder and she rushed for the stairs. She met her daughter coming down. 'Violet, are you all right?'

'Sure I'm all right. Just got missed by the biggest rock you've ever seen.'

CHAPTER 20

'Stay back, everyone,' said Edouard. 'I will go up.' He ascended the stairs and when he reappeared he was carrying a rock in both hands. It was the size of a medium loaf. Edouard came back down the stairs and let it fall on to the rush matting covering the floor. The noise left no doubt as to its weight.

'Where the hell did that come from?' said Hiram Sidewinder.

'It came over from the trees, from the jungle,' said Violet Sidewinder.

'Good God,' said Jolyon Downside to me. 'That's fifty metres and that thing must weigh twenty pounds. Can they do that, alone?'

'I don't know, I suppose so. They are very, very strong. I have never seen one do that before. Certainly they throw things. Normally quite small things, fruit, small stones, but that, I've never seen that.'

As I was speaking another huge crash came from the balcony, followed by more muted sounds from the thatch above. The next volley of rocks, all similar in size, struck the furniture barricade. Splinters of wood flew from the upturned dining table. The next rock broke the back of the dresser.

'There goes the barricade,' said Hiram Sidewinder as two more missiles smashed two lower chairs. 'My God, take cover. Stay this side of the building, stay this side of the building.

Randy, Josh, move those sofas and those chairs. If they come over that barricade this is where we must draw a line.'

We all obeyed. From a small enclave against the canvas we watched another boulder strike the balcony with a huge crash.

'My gun,' said Winnie Sidewinder, 'I've got to get my gun.' Her rifle was propped against the shattered dining table. 'I'll go and get it quickly.'

'No, Winnie, no,' cried Hiram Sidewinder.

But it was too late. Winnie Sidewinder ran across the room, snatched up her rifle and was halfway back when a rock struck her on the side of the head. For a moment she actually appeared to straighten. Her back arched and her head tilted slightly as though she were inspecting the thatched ceiling. Her eyes were wide open and then rolled backwards before she sank on to the ground. The gun remained impossibly standing on its butt for a moment before it fell down beside its owner.

'My God,' cried Hiram Sidewinder as he rushed forward to her side, 'Winnie, Winnie.' Another rock sailed through the opening as he clasped his wife's shoulders. Randy and Josh Sidewinder joined their father and, between the three of them, they pulled their unconscious mother back to the canvas wall. 'Winnie, Winnie,' cried Hiram Sidewinder. 'Mom, Mom, cried the boys in unison. Violet Sidewinder let out a piercing shriek. The body remained inert. Hiram Sidewinder gave directions. 'Randy, Randy, chest compression, quickly. Josh, lift her legs, lift her legs, that's right.' While his sons went into the routine, he lowered his mouth on to his wife's lips and attempted to breathe life into her throat. After a few minutes he sat back and, as he did so, a stream of blood fell from the corner of Winnie Sidewinder's mouth. Father and sons sat silent for a moment before Hiram Sidewinder gave a single incoherent roar of rage. In an instant he was on his feet.

'They killed my wife, goddamn it, they killed my wife, she's dead, my wife is dead. Those animals, those animals, they killed my wife. She was just getting her gun.' He looked round wildly as though for reassurance. 'She was just getting her gun and they killed her. Those animals, they killed my wife. Right, right, okay, okay.' Hiram Sidewinder picked up his gun. 'Right, right, we'll see, we'll see.'

Sidewinder became a man possessed. Clasping his rifle before him, he charged through the barricade, faltered on the soft sand, then bounded forward, firing as he went. 'C'mon,' he cried, 'c'mon Dump, come out.'

Edouard and I cried out together. 'No, no . . .'

Hiram Sidewinder fast approached the fringe of the forest. As he ran we heard the crack of his rifle, five, six, seven shots, into the dense jungle. We heard him continue to call above the firing. 'All right, all right, come on out, come on.' He had fired twelve shots before the rock hit him in the chest. It caused him to stagger but he appeared briefly to have regained his momentum as the second struck him. It knocked him down with the rifle still held in his right hand. Two more rocks missed him, then a third struck his shoulder. A fourth hit his head. Still he remained on his knees. The rifle fell from his hands and briefly he raised both arms in a cruciform before he pitched slowly on to the sand.

'Dad, Dad,' cried Randy Sidewinder.

'Come on,' cried Josh.

'No!' shouted Edouard.

Drawn by the same impulse, the Sidewinder twins burst from the lodge and the crackle of automatic firing assumed a constant rhythm as they ran. Josh reached his father first, knelt on the sand, threw away his rifle and lifted one of his arms. Randy took the other arm but retained his rifle in one hand. Supporting their father on either side they began to drag him back towards the lodge. They had achieved perhaps ten metres when the next salvo struck them. The missiles appeared to come now from many angles. Randy Sidewinder lifted his gun and attempted to fire one-handed into the jungle. He went down when three rocks struck him simultaneously. Josh Sidewinder was dragged on to the sand when his father fell. He attempted to rise before collapsing under the increasing rain of missiles. The onslaught continued for some minutes before, as though by order, the bombardment ceased and the three motionless bodies remained on the soft sand.

CHAPTER 21

We moved forward, stood behind the furniture barricade and stared at the bodies, immobile on the white sand. No noises came from the jungle; no further rocks or projectiles came in our direction. Behind me I heard a click. Both Edouard and I turned and found John Boxe, camera held before his face, repeatedly operating the shutter. Edouard turned on him, his face contorted with rage, but I held out an arm.

'No,' I said, 'we have gone beyond that. Let him record it all.'

Claire was standing to my right. On my left I heard a sound like a cat, a soft mewing. I looked down at Violet Sidewinder. She was staring with wide and unblinking eyes at the bodies of her family, barely twenty metres away. The noise that she was making slowly increased. I was about to reach for her when Cindy Applebloom came between us. All sign of panic had left her face as she enfolded the child in her arms. Speaking to me above Violet's head, she said: 'She is in deep shock. Leave her to me.' Gently she half led, half carried Violet Sidewinder to the far side of the lodge, against the canvas wall. She took one of the remaining chairs and sat with the girl in her arms, rocking slowly and murmuring into her ear.

I turned back to Claire, who had been joined by Jolyon Downside. They were both staring at the jungle and Downside said: 'Oh my God, look at that.' All along the edge of the forest black figures emerged on to the white sand. From inside the lodge our view was restricted to an area of barely one hundred metres at the edge of the trees. It was beginning to fill with chimpanzees. Behind them, the branches swayed as more pushed forward into the sunlight.

'Christ,' said Jolyon Downside, 'there are hundreds of them.'

Slowly they advanced on the lodge. Many, I saw, carried rocks in their hands, some had branches. The majority adopted the classic swinging walk of the primate, on hands and knuckles. Others, however, were slower moving, upright and walking on their hind legs. In a ragged line they advanced as far as the Sidewinders' bodies. Here they came to a halt. So far they had come in silence. The only sound was from the movement of sand, churned and pushed by feet and hands. At that moment I heard from the forest the beginnings of a now familiar sound. At first it came from a single voice, '*Humph, humph, humph.*' It then spread along the lines of chimpanzees. Within seconds the entire assembly had taken up the call and bodies began to move, barely perceptibly, to the repetition of the sound. '*Humph, humph, humph.*'

Then he came. The chimpanzees immediately surrounding the bodies on the beach fell back and he advanced out of the jungle. At first I did not recognise him. I had last seen him when he was thirteen years old. Big and ferocious he was but not then fully grown. Now at twenty-three years of age he was huge. At first he touched the ground lightly with his arms but then, when a pathway opened for him, he stood at full height and walked forward. He maintained the distinctive rolling motion of the walking ape but his shoulders were different. They were not hunched forward in the classic posture which allows for immediate charge or retreat. His shoulders were pulled back and his arms swung slowly by his side. Apart from his size, two things marked him immediately. His upper lip was drawn back, revealing a thin line of teeth. It was the expression that I had recorded ten years before. But I also recognised the wound inflicted by my own panga at that time. The slash of the blade had passed across his forehead. The copious blood which had then erupted from the cut had left a trail through the jungle that had persuaded us all of his death. Now I saw that it had healed but the hair had not fully returned. In order to compensate much longer hair had grown across the top of the temple. In the wind it floated outwards, giving the impression of a prominent peak jutting from the top of his head. It hung just above his eyes. As I watched him he raised a hand and swiped it aside, an irritated gesture as though swatting a troublesome insect from his sight. I stared at him and a tremor passed through my body. I felt Claire's hand link through my arm. 'Dump,' I said, 'it's him.'

Beside me the camera of John Boxe clicked incessantly. I turned to him and nodded. 'Go on, get it all or no one will believe it.'

Jolyon Downside said, 'My God, he's enormous, absolutely enormous.'

Dump made his way slowly towards the bodies on the sand. I noticed he was silent and did not join the surrounding orchestrated cacophony which now grew in pitch and volume. '*Humph, humph, humph.*'

When he reached the Sidewinders' bodies he paused, straightened, then looked to his left and his right. It was a theatrical gesture. I glanced at Downside, who was shaking his head. 'Shakespearean,' he muttered.

Dump had yet to look directly at the lodge. Now, as part of the same elaborate gesture, he lifted his head and gazed straight at me.

Across fifteen metres of beach eye contact was maintained for fully half a minute before I saw his upper lip curl further away from his teeth. I could make out the grinding of his jaw. Suddenly he thrust out an arm and pointed directly at my head. Around him the chorus grew still greater in pitch and volume. He dropped his gaze and then peered downwards at the Sidewinders' bodies. Hiram Sidewinder had fallen forward on to the sand. Dump lowered his own face until it reached a point two feet above Sidewinder's back. Then, with apparent ease, he extended a hand under the body and flipped it over. He stared down, his eyes within inches of the dentist's head. Beside me Claire closed her eyes.

'Oh my God,' she said, 'this is going to be terrible.'

Beside her Jolyon Downside spoke, his voice thick with fear. 'What is he going to do?'

On the beach Dump had taken hold of Sidewinder's head. Gently, he pulled it backwards and forwards and the whole body jerked upwards. As we watched another two chimpanzees came forward and picked up the inert body.

'God,' said Edouard, 'God, I can't watch this.'

In that instant I knew precisely what we needed to do. I turned to Edouard and said: 'Torch it, burn it.'

'Pardon? Burn it? What?'

'The lodge, burn the lodge, burn all of it.'

As Edouard shook his head, I said: 'It's the only way that we can make ourselves some time, don't you see? As soon as he's finished with the body, those chimpanzees are going to come for us. They are, Edouard, they are. But they will not enter a burning lodge. They are terrified of fire.'

Claire's voice came from behind me. 'But what about us? We will burn in here?'

'It will take time. It gives us time; don't you see? We need time. It will give us refuge at the back, and we can wait until the last minute.'

Claire looked at me. 'And if the boat has not arrived by then?'

'Then we must do all that we can. Run for the jetty. Don't you see it's our only chance?'

Downside was nodding his head. 'He's right. It's our only chance.'

I turned to Edouard. 'Have you got kerosene in here, for the lamps, for the lanterns?'

Edouard nodded. 'Two five-gallon cans, in there,' he said, pointing to the service area.

'Right, get them. Edouard, will you pour one of the cans on the barricade? It is useless as it is, they will tear it down in seconds, but not if it is on fire. Jolyon,' I said, 'can you bring the other one upstairs? Claire, the books, you have already made one pile, we must make two. All the books, quickly, quickly, let's get this done.'

'What would you like me to do?' The question came from John Boxe. He was gripping his camera like a man possessed.

'Are you all right?' I said.

'All right?' he said. 'I'm fine, perfectly fine.' He gave me a smile which made him appear to be on the verge of madness. 'I wanted to be a war photographer but I've got asthma.'

I gripped him by both shoulders. 'Keep that camera rolling, keep it rolling. Take everything. How much film have you got?'

'Oh,' he said, smiling, 'lots. Four hundred pictures left at least.'

As we spoke, Jolyon Downside came past me with the kerosene and we both climbed the stairs to the library. Together we started to hurl thirty years of discarded literary works into a pile in the centre of the floor. 'More, more,' I said. Together we managed huge armfuls of books and the pile grew. 'Now,' I said, 'now, the kerosene.' While I tore down the remaining books Downside upended the five-gallon can of kerosene over the pile that Claire had assembled at the far end of the library. When he had finished, he crossed to me and emptied the remainder on to the heap I had assembled. Kerosene spread in streams across the floor and began to drip down the stairs.

'Right,' I said, 'torch it, torch it now.' Boxes of matches lay on each of the tables for the ignition of the kerosene lamps. I took one and Downside the other. As I passed the balcony I looked out on the scene below. The dismembering of the body was complete. The sand at Dump's feet was red with blood. Seeing me on the balcony, he raised the head of Hiram Sidewinder and, in an unmistakable gesture, pointed with the other hand straight at me. I turned and shouted into the lodge, 'Light it now.' The ignition of Jolyon Downside's pile came first. Paperbacks burn more easily and the kerosene had been liberally applied. For a second it burned close to floor level and then burst into a huge tower of flame.

I stood above the second pile while Claire prepared to strike the match. On top of the heap my own image on the back of *The Prototype Primate* stared at me. On impulse I snatched it up and nodded to her. Seconds later Claire's pile of books began to burn. They were academic texts in hard covers or leather binders and took longer, but within a minute they also erupted. Flames leaped towards the thatched roof above. From below the staircase I heard Jolyon shout in triumph and when I ran down, still clutching my book, I saw that the barricade had become a wall of flame. Through it I saw Dump, his teeth now bared in the atavistic signal of anger and threat.

Claire and Jolyon descended the stairs. Edouard and John Boxe joined us in the middle of the dining room, which was now filling with smoke.

'How long do you think we've got?' said Boxe.

I turned, shrugged and managed to smile. 'I don't know. I've never torched a building before. I've never burned a thousand textbooks. I tend to write them, not burn them. I've no idea. Half an hour, maybe less.'

Edouard had gone to the canvas wall of the lodge, facing the lake. Slowly he unzipped one of the panels to provide a view of the shoreline and the jetty, some forty metres distant. Our way to the jetty was clear but there was no boat. Edouard had taken his field glasses from the bar. He scanned the horizon and shook his head.

'We can only hope,' he said.

CHAPTER 22

The whole of our group was now pressed back against the canvas wall. In front of us and above us the fire grew. The kerosene which had fallen on the staircase ignited and the bannister began to burn. We were trapped against the wall and, beyond that, against the lake. Through the gaps in the flames and through the entrance to the bar it was possible to catch glimpses of the beach and the jungle beyond. The black figures of the chimpanzees appeared to be growing in number. Otherwise they remained motionless, unwilling to move closer to the blazing lodge. The sounds of their cries had diminished but could still be heard through the sound of the fire. '*Humph, humph, humph.*'

I looked at our little group, now fellow refugees, fugitives, and I reflected even then on the vagaries of chance. It was, I thought, strange and wonderful company in which to die. The canvas flap remained slightly open and through it the sun illuminated the noble features of Jolyon Downside, a face known to millions as John Trotter in the *Trotter Files*. Behind him, on a chair, Cindy Applebloom, recent co-star of *Roger*, gently nursed a catatonic twelve-year-old, the last survivor of the Sidewinder family.

Claire approached, knelt beside them and mouthed silently, 'How is she?' Cindy Applebloom nodded and mouthed back, 'Asleep I think.'

Edouard had found a bench, on which he sat leaning back against the canvas. Silently he watched the destruction of thirty years of his life, years of scholarship and liberal endeavour, burning to allow his own escape. Only John Boxe appeared actively engaged, occasionally moving out into the heat in the centre of the hall, his Leica held out before him like the cross of a martyred saint. I picked up Edouard's binoculars and again scanned the horizon. No boat could be seen this side of the furthest headland, five kilometres away across the silver lake.

As I turned Edouard gave an agonised cry. '*Mon Dieu, mon Dieu*, look at that.' He pointed upwards to the atrium, to the apex of the thatch. The underside had now caught; the upper layer had been soaked by the recent storm but below it the thickly woven grass had become dry as tinder. It had caught suddenly in three places. As I watched, one of them exploded through into the daylight beyond. Showers of sparks and burning grass plummeted down on to what furniture remained and small fires began across the room. The hole created by the burning of the thatch released a new blast of air into the smouldering roof space. This caused sudden ignitions and then repeated explosions as the entire roof was engulfed in flame. On the beach beyond I saw the lines of chimpanzees move backwards. Some I saw beating at their fur as sparks, driven by the wind, fell on to the beach and the fringes of the jungle.

'What about them?' said Jolyon Downside. 'What's going to happen to them?' He was pointing at the three chimpanzees, now huddled back against the canvas, mouths open and emitting the familiar sound of panic and distress. '*Kuk, kuk, kuk.*'

I turned to Edouard. 'We must let them out. There is no other way. We can let them through the canvas flap and close it again.'

Edouard's eyes were dull, suddenly drained. 'If we let them out they will kill them. They will kill them before they kill us.'

'They can take their chance. If they are shielded by the lodge they can reach the edge of the forest before they are caught.'

'And then?' said Edouard.

'And then, they don't have a chance. They are all injured and one of them has a useless arm. But they can't stay here. The fire is terrifying them.'

Edouard recovered. 'Very well,' he said. He rose and unzipped the canvas flap to its extremity and held it wide open, an obvious invitation to escape. I approached the chimpanzees, imitating the call as best I could while flapping both arms in the direction of the now visible beach. '*Kuk, kuk, kuk,*' I said. 'Go now, go now.'

Brutus remained where he was, one arm swinging without volition by his side. Ajax and Horatio rose and started to move towards the opening. From the gap in the canvas they looked out at the beach and the lake beyond. Then they both turned and retreated back to the canvas wall, where they crouched once more.

'My God, they're too frightened,' said Edouard.

The heat at the back of the lodge was becoming intense. Edouard had brought three water bottles and we, like our three apes, crouched close to the floor where the smoke was thinner. The ceiling above the far end of the bar gave way and, with a fearful crash, descended on to the cedar floor. The fallen debris brought another eruption of flame and flecks of scorched and burning paper were now driven by the wind from the entrance of the bar. Within seconds we were covered by them. The recognisable remains of scholarship and research coated the floor, and ourselves, in a ghostly pall of white ash.

'We can't hold out much longer,' said Jolyon Downside and, on cue, Violet Sidewinder woke, sat bolt upright and stared, her eyes vacant at the disintegrating surroundings. The heat was now intense. Over half the floor area in what had been the dining and sitting areas was now ablaze. Through the canvas doorway I could see that the beach was still clear and that the causeway and jetty, forty metres away, remained unoccupied and intact. But there was still no boat. The sleeve of Edouard's jacket was burning – it had caught one of the sparks which fell in increasing numbers from the ceiling above us. He beat the fire out with his right hand, then turned to me.

'You and Claire go first with Cindy and the child, then John Boxe, then Jolyon and finally me.' As he spoke there was a sudden increase in the volume of noise from the chimpanzees, indicating a definite approach. '*Humph, humph, humph.*'

'Right,' said Edouard. In one pull he opened the flap. Daylight and air flooded into the back of the burning lodge, triggering another eruption of flame.

Cindy Applebloom set out across the beach, part leading, part carrying Violet Sidewinder. Claire looked at me. I nodded and touched her on the shoulder and she was gone. John Boxe followed her, still, impossibly, holding his camera behind him to capture the burning building he had just left. I became aware that I still had *The Prototype Primate*. I gripped it tight to my side and prepared to leave. Before I could do so Jolyon Downside stopped me.

'I still have this,' he said and held up the revolver. 'I do not know how to use it but it has five bullets remaining in the chamber. It is only if . . .' He paused. I nodded and followed Claire across the white sand. Behind me I heard Jolyon Downside and finally

Edouard leave the lodge and begin the agonising slow journey through soft sand towards the jetty. From the trees I heard the volume of the sounds increase yet again.

CHAPTER 23

I was making slow progress. When the gangway to the jetty was barely twenty metres away I was passed by Edouard, moving faster on my right-hand side. When he was a little ahead he gave a cry of pain and fell full length on to the sand. I stopped beside him.

'It's my ankle, my bloody ankle.'

Jolyon Downside had stopped immediately behind us. 'Come on, Edouard,' I said. 'Come on, for Christ's sake.' Discarding my book I held him under one arm and managed to lever him into an upright position. Downside immediately took the other and we pulled Edouard over the remaining distance.

The gangway which led to the jetty was some three metres wide and twenty metres long. It rose in a gradual ascent towards the jetty itself, a construction of wood and iron about ten metres square. On its shore side there were a number of benches for the convenience of visitors and on one of these Edouard collapsed. I turned back for the first time towards the lodge. It was an awesome sight. The thatch was now all ablaze. Sparks and burning wood exploded and floated upwards thirty metres into the air before being caught by the wind and driven back towards the forest. As I looked at the beach beneath us an extraordinary sight met my eyes. The black figures of two hundred chimpanzees were now spread out along the sand between the foot of the gangway and the blazing lodge. They were again in full cry. '*Humph, humph, humph.*' Many stood, others crouched, all were looking up towards us. Many bared their teeth, while from the throat the universal shout continued. '*Humph, humph, humph.*'

Despite the danger I confess to a deep sense of shock. I had lived with chimpanzees, studied them, researched their lives, was sometimes tempted to imitate their sounds and their movements. I had seen them hunt and kill. I had seen them on the extremes of anger and submission. I had watched them play and I had watched them die, slowly, secretly of old age, but I had never witnessed a manic mass exhibition such as this. Fear, raw, atavistic fear, tightened my throat. It interfered with my breathing, causing me to struggle and gasp while gripping the jetty's handrail for support.

Claire was by my side. 'What's the matter? You can't breathe?'

'No, no,' I shook my head. 'Is everybody here?'

'Yes,' she said, 'at the far end of the jetty.'

'Look at that,' I said, 'just look at that.'

I pointed to the end of the gangway where it met the beach itself. It was secured into the sand by solid stanchions and ropes which were themselves secured on to concrete blocks. At this point, on the gangway and barely two metres from the sand, three figures stood facing the army of chimpanzees. Ajax was on the left, Brutus to the right and, between them, Horatio stood upright, arms raised above his head, the classic sign of aggression in the male chimpanzee. Opposite them, on the beach, the numbers gradually increased. As I watched those in the front suddenly rushed forward in a mock charge. Horatio held his ground, Ajax dropped into a crouch and also charged.

The opposing sides came up short, a matter of feet away from each other. From the chimpanzees massing behind and facing the gangway the sounds gave way to the familiar shriek of the hunting chimpanzee; the hunt for blood.

I turned to look at the rest of the party. 'Right,' I said, 'they have given us time to breathe but that is all. Within minutes they will overwhelm them and will be on this jetty. The only way out is through the water. How long the boat will be we don't know but with luck we may stay afloat until that time. Chimpanzees will not follow us into the water.'

Violet Sidewinder, still tightly held by Cindy Applebloom, spoke in a small, dull voice. 'I can't swim,' she said.

After a pause, Cindy Applebloom said, 'Neither can I.'

Jolyon Downside raised the pistol he brought from the lodge. 'Then I will stay too,' he said.

'Very well,' I said, 'I speak only for myself, but I am not leaving without everyone.'

On the beach the hunting cries had were rising. The great mass of chimpanzees, an inexorable wave, moved forwards towards the three at the bottom of the gangway. I felt one of Claire's arms around my waist and I looked down at her face and smiled.

'What a way to go. At least we have managed to rewrite the whole of primate research.'

She smiled back, suddenly calm. '*Roger* will be a sellout,' she said; 'think of the publicity photographs.' She turned once more to the beach and then froze. 'My God,' she said, 'look at that, look at that.'

As I focused on the burning lodge I saw a figure on the still intact lakeside balcony, a figure huge and awesome against the background of the blazing building. Dump lifted both arms, threw back his head and gave a shriek. It was a hunting call but it carried with it an air of manic triumph. After a pause, it came again. It was the sound of a universal language, the final clarion call for bloody and triumphant battle. As he raised his arms again I saw that he carried an object in his right hand. At fifty metres I recognised the cover of *The Prototype Primate*. He shook it briefly above his head then grasped it in both hands and tore it to shreds. Caught in the heat of the fire the severed pages drifted upwards into the smoke. Then, slowly, he lowered his arms, took hold of the balustrade and, with one mighty heave, rent it apart and threw the wooden pieces on to the beach beneath. He then slowly turned, the curl of his lip clearly visible as he revolved.

'God,' I said, 'God, he's going to do it. A final act of contempt.' Claire added: 'The signal to attack.'

Slowly Dump, with his back towards us, lowered himself into a squatting position. He calmly settled his weight on both legs at precisely the moment that the balcony collapsed. The flames which had destroyed the supports suddenly burst upwards to consume the canvas sheets. Dump disappeared into the inferno below.

As the canvas disintegrated before our eyes, a terrible figure could be seen rising from the wreckage, now a mass of flame beneath the balcony itself. He was a flaming giant, an effigy fully alight while tufts of burning hair floated into the dancing light. There was one final mighty shriek and then the figure disappeared from view.

CHAPTER 24

After the shriek which marked the termination of Dump a profound silence fell across the beach.

Slowly it was filled with noises far more familiar to the ear of a primate researcher. The '*humph, humph*' had disappeared. It was gradually replaced by the many and varied sounds of primate life, instructions and demands relating to the provision of food or shelter or company. I heard it as one would welcome a boy's song rising from the desolation of battle. Slowly it spread across the beach. Family groups, indistinguishable minutes before, began to reform. Young chimpanzees, doubtless kept hidden in the forest, began to emerge to familiar parental calls and chiding.

Immediately at the foot of the gangway the centre of confrontation remained. Ajax, Horatio and Brutus stood within feet of forty chimpanzees who still displayed a perceptible air of threat. As I watched I heard Cindy Applebloom shout behind me.

'The boat,' she cried, 'the boat.'

I turned and with an indescribable, sense of giddy relief saw the lodge boat round the nearest promontory, less than a kilometre in the distance. They had obviously held to a path close to the shoreline rather than risk the centre of the lake. As it drew closer I saw the figures of Benedict and Boniface standing on the prow, both of them scanning the beach and the jungle behind. From the remaining crew in the boat I heard shouts of alarm at the sight of the burning lodge and soon all four appeared at the prow. When I turned to the beach I saw a sight which has remained imprinted on my memory ever since. Barely half of the chimpanzees remained. Those that did were making steadily for the fringe of the jungle. Some went individually, some were now in family groups. Those closest to the foot of the gangway had turned their backs. Now scurrying on all fours, they rapidly covered the sixty metres of white sand and disappeared into the forest. By the time the boat arrived at the jetty, the flaming lodge and the bodies of three human beings and one female chimpanzee were the only remaining testament to carnage.

The boat, as Edouard had promised, was the first of two. The second, carrying a squadron of Tanzanian Park Rangers, was expected the following day. Plans were now made for embarkation. The boat carried a full kit of emergency medicine. From this Cindy Applebloom selected a strong sedative, which she administered to Violet Sidewinder. The child then fell into a deep sleep. She also found bandages and a makeshift splint for Edouard's ankle and it was decided that he would accompany us back in the boat to Akawi.

Jolyon Downside and I, with Benedict and Boniface, then carried out the task of assembling the bodies of the Sidewinders and recovering the head of Yojo Bo Fang, which had been stored in the kitchen freezer. The kitchen building, in the jungle, had remained untouched. Despite the obvious need for forensic examination and investigation, it was decided the bodies could neither remain on the beach nor be carried back in our boat. They were, therefore, placed on the kitchen table and covered by blankets. The head of Hiram Sidewinder was never found, nor was the body of Yojo Bo Fang. Possibly, many, many years hence, they will be discovered separately in the jungle and will be the subject of much learned disputation.

After the retreat of the hostile chimpanzees, Ajax, Horatio and Brutus had waited a short while and then also had disappeared, without farewell, into the jungle.

The four of us buried Gertrude's body in a shallow grave before Jolyon and I returned to the boat. Benedict and Boniface were to remain on duty, in charge of the lodge, until Edouard returned with the Park Rangers the following day.

We all embarked on the boat a little after noon. Claire and I took up residence on the prow. Edouard sat in the cabin at the rear, in deep conversation with Jolyon Downside and Cindy Applebloom. John Boxe took valedictory pictures of the receding lodge from the stern. We all helped ourselves from the bar. Claire and I drank whisky, Jolyon Downside, Edouard and John Boxe drank beer and Cindy Applebloom poured herself a substantial gin and tonic. For a while there was an extraordinary illusion of normality as the boat ploughed its way along the forested shoreline towards a far-off civilisation.

'Do you think,' said Claire, 'that we should write an account now while everything is clear and fresh? There is bound to be a serious investigation and we will obviously be prime witnesses.'

'Do you know,' I said, 'I don't think I could write a word, and as for remaining fresh in the mind, I can think of nothing that could interfere with this memory for many, many years.'

She smiled. 'You were great,' she said, 'for a professor; decisive. If we hadn't fired the lodge we would not have survived.'

She drank her whisky, contemplating the receding shore, then she said, 'And what will the world make of Ronald Dump? It is bound to cause a massive sensation. He has completely rewritten the whole of primate research, the whole of our branch of anthropology, of behavioural studies, now all consigned to history.

'It goes further than that,' she said, still musing. 'The whole liberal assumption, the noble savage in the benign wilderness, all gone, all destroyed by Ronald Dump. And what will become of the apes, what will become of the Serole mountains? Have they won their revolution?'

I answered her question. 'No, they have not and you know that as well as I. The Chinese will continue to log their forests. They are utterly ruthless and completely unstoppable. Chimpanzees may have the strength of three men but it avails them absolutely nothing without the two per cent of missing DNA. They will end up in a tiny area, something resembling a zoo. And incidentally, I think that's why they attacked us. I don't believe your Chinese theory. I don't believe that they knew Yojo Bo Fang was there, any more than I believe they read his maps. Dump came after us because he knew that he could. As Winnie Sidewinder said, we were the wet liberals. All books and Botticelli. But like the loggers, we're human. We were a soft target. When they destroyed us, destroyed Edouard, destroyed the research, destroyed the wet liberals, then, in reality, they were destroying themselves because without us they have no value, no *raison d'être*.'

'Except to be shot and turned into trophies,' said Claire.

'Ah, yes, Hiram Sidewinder's theory, placing a value on killing. That won't work either. If you allow the hunting of chimpanzees it simply feeds the appetite. When Hiram Sidewinder and a thousand dentists in America have shot them all out of the wilderness, those left in the zoos will wish their heads were on waiting-room walls.'

Claire got up and finished her drink. 'God, we are being maudlin. We're alive, aren't we? I'm going to get another couple of those.'

'I'll come with you,' I said, 'it's getting wet out here.'

We both walked to the cabin area at the stern of the boat, past Jolyon Downside and Cindy Applebloom carrying their drinks to the seats which gave a changing view of the jungle and the mountains beyond. They also appeared deep in thought and we passed with barely a nod. In the cabin we found Edouard sitting at a table.

CHAPTER 25

Edouard poured the drinks and set them on the table.

I said, 'Before we drink together, both Claire and I want to say something. This has been a terrible tragedy for all of those that have lost their lives but also for you. You have lost everything that you have worked for, everything that you have built up, all the priceless learning and knowledge that you have accumulated over so many years, all gone. I want to say that Claire and I are very sorry indeed.'

Edouard acknowledged this with his raised glass and we solemnly drank together.

'Yes, well,' said Edouard, setting down his whisky, 'I have been thinking about that and it's really what I wanted to talk to you about. Everything may not be quite as bad as you obviously believe. It rather depends on how we report things when the investigation begins.'

I found myself staring at him in blank amazement. Claire's face mirrored my own.

'Edouard,' I said, 'I simply don't understand what you are saying. This has been the most terrible tragedy, not only for those involved but also for the whole of academic research, learning. When the world learns about Dump and what has occurred here, there will be the most massive repercussions.'

'Yes,' said Edouard, 'I think I understand that, of course. But, how can I put this? I wonder if it is really necessary for Dump to come out at all?'

'What!'

'Now, hear me out, please. Why should anyone, the world that is, need to know about Dump? He is, after all, dead and now we know that he is really dead, burnt to a cinder. So Dump is all over, is no more. Certainly he was a malign influence. You, I know, believed him to be a psychopath, insofar as such things can exist in chimpanzees. But he is all over, he's dead.'

'But so,' said Claire, as she briefly counted on her fingers, 'so are eight human beings. All need to be accounted for. Dump killed them all, either directly or indirectly, in the most brutal circumstances. How can that simply be forgotten? How can he be . . . airbrushed out of history?'

'Well, yes, if we could just consider the eight people who you say are dead, or rather who *are* dead. They were probably killed by Dump. Let us just consider them for a minute; first we have the Bellingham sisters.'

'And Moses.'

'Yes, and Moses of course, who is missing. The Bellingham sisters, if we could just consider them. As you know, we get information on all our guests in case there is an emergency, including next of kin and other relevant details. I looked closely at the Bellingham sisters before they arrived. It is sometimes a good idea to find out if guests are people of substance who might leave some small bequest to the lodge. Anyway, the Bellingham sisters are, were, spinsters and have no immediate relatives. I happen to know because they told me when they were setting off on their trip. I happen to know that they have left all their available money to a donkey charity. No doubt the donkey charity will be very grateful, probably more grateful than it would be than having the Bellingham sisters as volunteers. So no one is going to make a fuss about them. Why should they? Of course, it will be necessary to say that they went missing. This has happened before and can be ascribed to many things: accident, avalanche, rock fall.'

'Avalanche? Rock fall?'

'Yes, you know, a ravine; the weather was pretty bad. Anyway the point that I am making is that no one is going to enquire too closely, it will pass over. Then, of course, there is Moses. Moses was getting on a bit, in his forties. His children, I know, are all grown up and he very rarely saw his wife. I would propose making a substantial gift to the family. They will be more than happy, I assure you, more than happy. That rather removes the Bellinghams and Moses. In other words, three out of eight.'

'But we know they were murdered by Dump.'

'No, we don't. No, no, we don't. We don't know what they would say if they were alive. It may not have been Dump at all. They may say they have been murdered by somebody else.'

'Good God, Edouard,' I said, 'I don't believe that I'm hearing this. But even suppose you are right, that is three out of eight. What about Yojo Bo Fang?'

'Ah, yes, Yojo Bo Fang. You see, who was Yojo Bo Fang? Hmm? Yojo Bo Fang, we know, was an imposter and, as an imposter, was almost certainly travelling under an assumed name. He never gave me his passport although it is required by Tanzanian law. He told me that it would be sent by the university. I am willing to bet a great deal of money that there is no such university. Yojo Bo Fang was a logger, a Chinese logger. He is, or was, the very devil incarnate. The Chinese logging company are hardly likely to make a fuss about Yojo Bo Fang. How could they? Yojo Bo Fang does not exist.'

'His remains are here.'

'Well, not much of him. There's a head, certainly, but all the rest has gone and there wouldn't even be a head if you hadn't brought it back in that file box. But, never mind, there is a head, I grant you. A head, may I say,' Edouard paused and looked straight at me, 'a head without spectacles. If there were to be any kind of investigation the authorities might want to know *what happened to his spectacles?* So the only people alive who know about Yojo Bo Fang's head are the people on this boat.'

'And Benedict and Boniface.'

'Ah, yes, Benedict and Boniface. Yes, well, you see, I have had a word with Benedict and Boniface. I have told them precisely who Yojo Bo Fang is, or was, namely that he was a Chinese logger. Benedict and Boniface regard Chinese loggers as being rather lower than bum fleas, you know, that chimpanzees get in the anus. I did say that if Yojo Bo Fang's head was to disappear then no questions would be asked and it would be associated with a substantial increment in wages.'

I sat speechless whilst Edouard beamed at me across the table.

'Can I get you another drink?' he said. Claire and I looked at each other and nodded our heads, struck dumb.

While he fetched the liquor, he said: 'I know this may all sound a bit surprising but it has occurred to me, only very recently, that quite a lot of these events may in fact be blessings in disguise. Now,' he said, returning the drinks to the table, 'I know what you are going to say next, you are going to say "The Sidewinders."'

'The Sidewinders,' said Claire and I together.

'Yes, there you are, I said that you would. Now I also know

a little about the Sidewinders. You know a little too. Hiram Sidewinder is, was, a dentist so he has a lot of patients but he does not have an awful lot of kin. His parents are dead and he has two brothers, both hunters. Winnie Sidewinder is an orphan. Now the Sidewinder brothers have not spoken to each other for ten years. How do I know this? Because it is legend within the American hunting fraternity, some of whom have occasionally come to stay at the lodge. Hiram Sidewinder and his brothers fell out very badly over a moose, that is to say the animal with horns. They were on a hunting trip together and Hiram Sidewinder shot the moose or, at least, he said he did. His brothers claim that they shot the moose after Hiram had merely winged it. Like most American families they are extremely litigious. The whole thing ended up in the district court in Wyoming. That was where they shot the moose. The district judge found in favour of Hiram Sidewinder's brothers, which involved a finding that Hiram had failed to finish off his kill, apparently a considerable *faux pas*. Hiram Sidewinder's standing is pretty low in Wyoming and he hasn't spoken to his brothers since. Indeed, it is thought that they were responsible for posting the giraffe picture on the internet where it has gone viral.'

'And young Violet?'

'Ah, yes, I was coming to little Violet. Violet, we know, is in a catatonic state. When she recovers she is likely only to have a deeply imperfect memory of what happened to her parents. Her mother, we know, has been burnt to a crisp in the fire, so that much is a matter of agreement.'

Edouard held up his hand against my interruption. 'What about the other Sidewinders? All dead and one without a head. Now, this is the clever part and may need a little help from the

Tanzanian coroner but it will only be a little help and easily obtained. The Sidewinders, as we know, are manic hunters. This is what occurred. They came to the lodge ostensibly for some rest and relaxation and to observe the chimpanzees. But they really came in order secretly to shoot them. Anyone who knows them will believe that. On the first day here, unbeknown to me, they used a duplicate key to obtain access to their gun box, which was officially under my control. They took a number of guns, locked the box and made off into the forest. They are not used to hunting in jungle and they swiftly got lost. They were also obviously spooked by the sound of chimpanzees all around them. They became separated. What followed was a tragic hunting accident. Hiram Sidewinder, mistaking his sons for two chimpanzees, shot both in the head. When he came upon their bodies he was overcome with remorse and blew his own head off.'

Claire, I noticed, was sitting with her mouth wide open. I decided that a little levity was in order. 'Oh come on, come on, Edouard. Blew his own head off with a 407 bolt-action rifle? He's not only a mad hunter, he's a mad contortionist as well.'

Edouard smiled a condescending smile. 'Oh no, not with a 407 rifle, although, as a matter of interest, the 407 rifle is available with an empty magazine and with his fingerprints on the trigger.' His smile became one of grim satisfaction. 'No, no, he didn't blow his head off with a 407, he blew it off with this.' So saying, Edouard produced the revolver that Sidewinder had entrusted to Jolyon Downside. 'There it is. Hiram Sidewinder's fingerprints are all over it and there is one bullet used in the magazine.'

'But Edouard,' I said, 'when you put in a bullet in your brain, your head does not come off.'

'That's where the Tanzanian coroner comes in. On this occasion it did come off. Unusual, I know, but who knows what a good blast with a Smith and Wesson will do. The head, as you know, has never been recovered, only the body, and also the bodies of the two boys that were retrieved from the jungle following this tragic accident.'

'But the boys do not have bullets in their brains, they were hit by rocks. In both cases the side of the skull is shattered.'

'It is the easiest thing in the world to mistake one type of skull damage for the other, particularly if you are a Tanzanian coroner out on a boat trip and have consumed a considerable quantity of whisky. And a coroner who also could, quite rightly, expect a substantial fee.'

'But Violet . . .'

'Violet will naturally believe what she is told by people she will trust. If at any stage in her life she were to revert to the story of a gigantic mad ape tearing her father's head off, it would be, to say the least, very unlikely to be believed. But I do not anticipate any such thing happening. Hiram Sidewinder was insured for twenty million dollars and was hugely wealthy in his own right. The whole of that considerable fortune will be available to Violet Sidewinder, who will no doubt enjoy a life of conspicuous luxury telling people of her father's heroic death.'

There was a long pause, during which I carefully contemplated Edouard. At first I had thought that he had gone stark mad. Now I knew that he had not and I was beginning to get a glimmer of the next stage.

'And who, exactly, will Violet Sidewinder trust?'

'Ah,' said Edouard, 'a good question. Myself, of course, but most importantly Cindy Applebloom, who is, as you know, a famous British actor and a former nurse. Insofar as she needs corroboration it will be provided by Jolyon Downside. He, of course, is another famous British actor, best known for his role as John Trotter in the *Trotter Files*.'

'Are they in on this?'

'Absolutely. You see they are very worried indeed about the effect this publicity would have on *Roger*, the film, which is due to be released in about a week's time. Roger, as you know, is a beautiful ape and the recipient of a degree from Oxford. It is a very moving film. Indeed, you may remember the Bellingham sisters were moved to tears. If the press was to reveal that primates – or, at least, that one primate was a gigantic psychopathic ape who had attempted to kill both lead actors and everyone else, the effects on the film could be ghastly. Jolyon Downside has no recollection at all of seeing an ape called Dump, or any other apes for that matter. Cindy Applebloom is the same. So you see, that just leaves you, the pair of you, my old friends and fellow researchers.'

I looked at him over my whisky glass and said: 'I can't do this, Edouard. In addition to being outright perjury it is tantamount to academic heresy. After what has happened, to deny the existence of Dump, let alone the effect that he has had, would be to pervert the science to which I have dedicated my life.'

'Oh come on, said Edouard, suddenly angry, 'you didn't mention Dump in *The Prototype Primate*, did you?'

I felt defensive. 'No, I didn't but that was different.'

'It was different,' said Edouard, fixing me with a cold stare, 'because you had broken the rules. You had interfered in primate behaviour. You had damn near killed Dump and, of course, we all wish you had. But that's why he didn't appear in *The Prototype*

Primate. He was written out of science even though it was your view, not mine, that he was an aberrant psychopathic ape who would have deserved, at least, a footnote in an academic treatise.'

'That's partly true.'

'Partly true? It is completely true. If you can leave Dump out of *The Prototype Primate*, you can leave him out of this fucking carnage.'

Edouard could see that he was winning and pressed it home. 'What do you think will happen, Arthur, if you write *the truth*? If it is believed, it will cause mayhem. Chinese loggers will be able to shoot chimpanzees at will and claim that they were dangerous Dumps. The Serole Lodge will cease to exist. Tourism and research will cease to exist and, as a result, in a remarkably short period of time, primates, these primates, these chimpanzees, our first cousins, will cease to exist as well, except behind steel bars where they will be kept and looked at not as noble savages but as Dumps, *Ronald Dumps*.'

'I need to think about this.'

'No, you don't,' said Edouard, 'no you don't, you mustn't think about this. There is, in reality, only one choice.' He swung round to look at Claire. 'I'm right, aren't I?'

Claire took a long gulp of her whisky and then, energetically, nodded her head. She looked sideways at me. 'He's right. He's right, he is right. We don't have to have *seen* anything. The Bellinghams disappeared. We didn't see Yojo Bo Fang, we didn't see the Sidewinders on their hunting trip. But what,' she said, turning to Edouard, 'what about the fire?'

'What about that? That's the best bit. The lodge was insured in case of fire by accident. It was, of course, not insured for deliberately started fires. The insurance is not a huge sum but it is sufficient to rebuild the lodge with wonderful new facilities for guests and staff and,' he said, smiling at me, 'we can have a new research centre named after the famous author of *The Prototype Primate*.'

I could not resist a smile but said: 'No, Edouard, no, I am sorry, that is a step too far. To lie by omission in the service of the greater good is one thing, to receive accolades for it would be quite another.'

On my left, Claire intervened: 'Well,' she said, 'I don't know, I don't take the same view. I think the Claire Welbourne Research Centre will be very nice.'

I was surprised and a little shocked. I saw that she was staring at Edouard. Her eyes were shining.

I played a last card. 'Aren't we forgetting one fundamental and important person? What about John Boxe?'

'John Boxe? Oh, John Boxe,' said Edouard with a fine display of surprise, 'John Boxe, well, well, well. He, of course, is directly employed by the producers of *Roger*. In fact, he is employed by the director of *Roger*, who is, I think, called Robert Bellbottom. In fact, I have heard it said that he, Boxe, is Robert Bellbottom's lover. He has a contract and is entirely bound by confidentiality clauses. I don't think that is a real problem.'

'But what about his camera?' said Claire. 'He has a camera full of pictures, over four hundred pictures that tell the truth about the whole event. He may well be Bellbottom's lover now but what happens when they split up? It does happen, you know. He has the proof. It could be worth millions. No one would believe him without the pictures, but with the pictures no one could believe anything else.'

'Ah yes, the camera. I had forgotten.'

In the pause that succeeded this John Boxe put his head round the cabin door. 'I say,' he said, 'has anyone seen my camera?'

'Your camera?' said Edouard. 'Where did you leave it?'

'I'm sure I left it on a ledge at the back of the boat. I was taking the last pictures of the lodge.'

'Really?' said Edouard. 'And it's not there now?'

'I've asked the crew and I've asked everybody else.'

Edouard affected a look of deep concern. 'The ledge at the stern? Not that slippery mahogany ledge close to the edge of the wheelhouse?'

'I didn't think it was slippery. It seemed like a perfectly normal ledge to me.'

'Let's have a look,' said Edouard. 'I hope it is not the ledge I'm thinking of. We have lost stuff there before.' The two of them left and within minutes Edouard was back. He picked up his drink and contemplated the table.

'What a terrible thing,' he said; 'the young chap is really very upset. I think he is crying in the heads. All that work, all those records lost in the lake.' Edouard transferred his gaze to the cabin window. Beyond it the lake could be seen stretching into the far distance. The early afternoon sun glittered across the calm and even surface. 'What a shame,' said Edouard, 'what a shame.'

CHAPTER 26

Later, when we neared Akawi, Claire took up a position she had enjoyed many years before at the prow of the boat. As it turned the last promontory, the water always became rough and choppy. She stood and laughed in the spray as it soaked her hair and the denim jacket which she would later hang out to dry. As the boat neared its mooring, she came back into the cabin, dripping water into the last of her whisky. I smiled a half smile.

'Wet liberal,' I said.

She did not smile but looked at me with an expression I could not read.

'Perhaps,' she said. 'Perhaps not.'

CHAPTER 27

April 2019.

Letter from Dr Arthur Welbourne to Sir Adrian Fetherby

Adrian Fetherby
Director, Royal Geographical Society
Kensington Gore
London SW7

24 April 2019

Dear Adrian,

DUMP

As discussed briefly over the phone I am sending you a manuscript. It is in the narrative form and at present enjoys the title Dump *for reasons which you will quickly discover. It is a little over fifty thousand words. I anticipate that you will read it quickly and I will assume for the purposes of this letter that you have already done so. It is the true account of the destruction of the Serole Lodge in 2017.*

To my shame I have remained silent on this terrible event until now. Indeed I have colluded in the false story which attributes the fire to an accident involving the spillage of kerosene by a careless employee. I have also allowed the official account of the Sidewinders' hunting accident to go unchallenged.

I can remain silent no longer.

By now you will have received the news of my resignation from Oxford. In the academic press there has been speculation that I have made way for my wife to succeed to the Chair at St John's. Nothing could be further from the truth. My concealment of the events at Serole was a gross, possibly criminal, deception and represents a grotesque scientific calumny of the worst kind. I have entered into a conspiracy to conceal Dump from the world. In doing so I have hidden the fact that I intervened in conflicts between the chimpanzees and, in doing so, nearly killed the animal who was to assume the main role in the unimaginable events which followed. Not only were these events horrific in themselves, resulting in the deaths of eight human beings, but they mark a fundamental departure from our knowledge and assumptions relating to primate behaviour. They literally rewrite the bibles. The revelation that an entire region, an entire species could suddenly alter their habits, their collective personality, their mores, and indulge in such self-destructive, violent behaviour alters all our received wisdom that has been accepted for generations.

Now that I have decided to reveal the truth I could not possibly expect to retain my post let alone my self-respect. That is the reason that I have resigned. Far from leaving the Chair for my wife, I fervently hope that she does not get it. She is, has been, a co-conspirator. Worse, she has become the main architect of the deception. She and Edouard Deprès have rebuilt and revitalised the Serole Lodge with the proceeds, and on the basis, of a scientific lie. They have set up a research centre in her name with money from the insurance and have accepted lucre from the Chinese to enhance the institution and its terms of reference. The last body of research examines the potential of chimpanzees inhabiting forests that are 'sustainably' exploited for logging, the ultimate betrayal. While they have done this they have scarcely bothered to conceal the fact that they have become lovers, certainly not from me.

I have of course told Claire of my intention to reveal all of the truth. At first she was angry, then, after a long telephone conversation with Edouard, she laughed in my face. She called me barking mad. No one, she said, will believe in Dump. He is a monstrous figment of my imagination. There is not a shred of real evidence remaining. He is, she said, inherently incredible: a violent, psychopathic, sexually aberrant huge ape who led a basically non-aggressive, gentle species on a rampage of murder and destruction. It was all over, she said, just as Edouard had planned on that fatal boat.

It has not deterred me. When it is subjected to examination the truth, the whole truth will be believed. I think she knows it. But there is a wider truth that has occurred to me which troubles me more. It lies in the power that Dump possessed. It is not the brute strength, the crude violence, the sexual bullying, the aggressive leadership and the roaring arrogance. It is the power to corrupt otherwise good, liberal and decent people who would rather pretend he did not exist than confront his reality; people who will ultimately rationalise an awful phenomenon.

So, Adrian, now you know it all and I would like to enlist your support in a campaign to bring this to the world. I have sent my manuscript to George Tubrill, Environment Editor at the Guardian, who will have exclusive rights to publication. He has the resources to obtain the available evidence. I have also sent it to Hotspur Parts, who was my agent for the publication of The Prototype Primate.

As to your part, I would like to turn all this into a lecture at the RGS. It will of course deal with the events at Serole but also with the wider ethical, scientific issues raised by Dump with which I am now living. It should be fascinating. I would suggest November as a suitable date. I would of course be happy to meet to discuss the whole story. I now have plenty of leisure to do so!

Yours ever,

Arthur

CHAPTER 28

George Tubrill
Environment Editor
The Guardian
London N1
24 April 2019

Dear George,

DUMP

Following our recent telephone conversation I am enclosing a manuscript entitled Dump *which contains the true account of the destruction of the Serole Lodge in 2017. I also enclose a copy of a long letter which I have sent today to Adrian Fetherby at the Royal Geographical Society, an old friend like you. In addition to setting out my present position that letter deals with my strategy for the publication and revelation of the facts. It will, of course, be unpleasant, possibly dangerous, for me but I am determined on this course. I have lived under a cloud for two years and now experience a profound sense of relief.*

I am very happy to give you exclusive rights to the story and to the aftermath. It should cause quite a sensation.

I have carried out a certain amount of research and as a result can provide you with contact details for all the main players. These are Claire and Edouard, Jolyon Downside, Cindy Applebloom and John Boxe. Violet Sidewinder has been adopted. I have the name of the agency, which is unwilling to provide details. I doubt if she could assist much anyway. Unsurprisingly I have no details relating to Yojo Bo Fang. The Bellinghams appear to have had no relatives and few friends. Their house has been sold and the proceeds donated to the donkey charity they supported. Apart from gratitude the charity had little comment to make.

Over to you, old friend. You have the experience and expertise to create a sensational exclusive which will reveal Dump to the world. It should have happened long ago.

As ever,

Arthur

CHAPTER 29

Hotspur Parts
Parts, Bond and Vanquish, Literary Agents
Vision House
London E15
24 April 2019

Dear Hotspur,

DUMP

Following today's telephone call I am enclosing a manuscript entitled Dump. *It runs to a little over fifty thousand words and contains the true account of the destruction of the Serole Lodge in 2017. I also enclose a copy of a letter of today's date to Adrian Fetherby, Director of the Royal Geographical Society. The contents are self-explanatory.*

I well remember the fantastic job that you did for me with The Prototype Primate. *I do hope that you will do the same with* Dump. *I appreciate that Circumspect no longer exist as publishers but there must be many others who will publish this important document. I also understand that the events themselves may be too graphic, too horrific to appeal to an academic, or quasi-academic readership. However, I have in mind a substantial postscript or preface setting out the personal, ethical and moral dilemmas inherent in dealing with a phenomenon like Dump. They are very real and have been my constant companions for two years.*

Perhaps we could have lunch to discuss this?

I look forward to hearing from you shortly.

Best as ever,

Arthur

CHAPTER 30

THE ROYAL GEOGRAPHICAL SOCIETY
From the Director, Sir Adrian Fetherby

My dear Arthur,

DUMP

Thank you so much for sending me this absolutely fascinating manuscript. I have read it with great interest and have shared it with a number of my senior colleagues. What an adventure it must have been and what a terrifying character was Dump! We are all so happy that you survived.

Arthur, let me say straight away that I have boundless respect for you as a scientist and an academic. The publication of The Prototype Primate *was a seminal moment for anthropology. Certainly it was controversial in its conclusions and some harsh things were said by eminent people who should have known better. That was many years ago and we have all been delighted that your beliefs have been accepted as part of the mainstream of primate research. Your ten years at Oxford has demonstrated total commitment to your science and to your students. Many of them will remember you with affection and gratitude. They will be as sorry as we all are to hear of your resignation.*

Let me say that I, personally, have no problem accepting all that you say about Dump and the decisions that were taken to conceal the truth about him and the destruction of the lodge. It must have been very hard for you to live, for the last two years, under the burden that those decisions placed upon you. They have obviously put unbearable stress on you and on your marriage to Claire. The whole of academia was sorry to hear that you had parted. As you know, you were quite the golden couple of primate study. But we were, of course, unaware of the strains that you were both under.

So may I come to your 'campaign to bring this to the world'? I am very sorry to say that I am unable to assist in the way that you suggest. Despite my personal support the Board members are unanimously of the view that the problems of credibility are far too great, for three reasons. First, any audience would have to accept that three eminent scientists – yourself, Claire and Edouard – had entered into a conspiracy (your word) to conceal the truth. It would be difficult enough if there were a universal 'mea culpa'. However, Claire and Edouard emphatically deny that they have concealed anything. (As to the intimate relationship between them I obviously cannot comment.) The second problem involves accepting that hundreds, perhaps thousands of chimpanzees could collectively act totally contrary to the behaviour patterns of their species under the malign influence of Dump. Which brings me to the third reason, Dump himself. He is simply too awful to be credible. The ape you describe is not only violent, sexually aberrant and psychopathic, he is also cunning, scheming, manipulative and deranged. Even if chimpanzees were capable of collective action as you describe, it beggars belief that they would act in that way under the influence of such a monster.

All of that, I hasten to add, Arthur, is the view of the Board. As I say, I, personally, accept your account implicitly.

Finally I come to your request for an RGS lecture in September. The Board were unanimous in the view that a full lecture would simply be too stressful for you at this time. We (and this includes me) feel that a long period of rest and recuperation would do you the world of good. Next year, perhaps, we would consider a return to The Prototype Primate, *which would mark ten years since publication.*

My very best wishes as always,

Adrian

CHAPTER 31

Parts, Bond and Vanquish
Literary and Theatrical Agents

By post and email
15 May 2019

Dear Arthur,

DUMP

Thank you for sending me Dump. I read the manuscript with interest.

Let me say straight away that it requires a lot of work before I could consider placing it before a major publisher.

I have shown it informally to Felicity Fulbright, your old editor at Circumspect (now with Bergsgarten), and she agrees.

The first problem is where do we pitch this? It certainly will fail in the academic market. As you yourself say, it is just too graphic, too horrific to fall into that genre. Goodall and Fossey have both recorded acts of violence in their works on chimpanzees and gorillas but nothing approaching this. Gratuitously tearing off heads, legs and testicles represents a totally new departure in primate behaviour within the species. Decapitating Chinese researchers (all right, loggers) and stoning American dentists to death will certainly not fit on the anthropology shelves. You propose adding a postscript or preface dealing with the 'personal, ethical and moral dilemmas'. In my view that simply makes the problem worse. It gets us straight into psychology or even professional negligence, both very difficult niche markets.

Which takes us to fiction, and here again, how do we pitch this? It could be a disaster movie along the lines of Jaws. *There could be a sequel,* Dump 2 *(if he hadn't burnt to death). But it would need a complete rewrite. All the characters are, or were, real, including you. Also all the beheading and stoning gets a bit repetitive. One solution would be to turn it into some form of political allegory with Dump in the role of a nightmare politician. The problem here is that it's just too over the top. It would have to be an allegory for Uzbekistan or Albania and who gives a damn about them?*

That leaves the environment/climate change market. The problem is that it's just not cataclysmic enough. To sell anything here it's got to be global and immediate, pandemics, biblical floods, choking dust, nuclear disaster. I am afraid the Serole apes just don't figure.

I am sorry, Arthur, and also sorry to hear about Oxford and your marriage. Take some time and write another Prototype Primate, *much more your style.*

Best as ever,

Hotspur

From: Arthur.welbourne@batty.com
To: Parts@PBV.co.uk
16 May 2019

Hotspur, I received your letter and reply immediately. May I ask you to reconsider? It doesn't matter how it is pitched, science, psychology, professional negligence, fiction or climate change. This is a desperately important story and needs to be told.

    Arthur

CHAPTER 32

THE GUARDIAN

14 June 2019

Dear Arthur,

DUMP

As you know this has become something of a crusade. In the past two months I have done little else and even persuaded my reluctant editor to give me a modest budget.

I have been to Serole, spent a night at the lodge and interviewed Edouard. Claire was not there. I interviewed her separately in Battersea where she is now living. I also interviewed Jolyon Downside and Cindy Applebloom together on the set of Trotter Files *(ninth series). John Boxe refused to see me. He is living with Robert Bellbottom, who spoke to me on his intercom. He told me that Boxe has a confidentiality agreement with Bellbottom Films which lasts apparently for sixty years. He is not prepared to release him from it. Following the huge international success of* Roger *(it has become, as you know, a cult movie) he has more than enough money to ensure that Boxe does as he is told. Threats from the Guardian will be ineffectual.*

Edouard and Claire, interviewed separately, were near word-

perfect. Indeed whole paragraphs were identical. They are undoubtedly lying.

Of course I questioned them closely. The Bellinghams and Moses? 'Tragic, unsolved accident, bodies never found. There was a violent tropical storm that day. Moses would have taken shelter in a gully or ravine in which there was possibly a landslide. The Bellinghams would have clung to each other and to him; a terrible chain reaction.' It's all speculation and absolute rot. The Sidewinders? 'Dreadful hunting accident caused by their addiction to illegal shooting.' Hiram's head? 'Blown off with a Smith and Wesson; a very rare event but accepted by the Tanzanian coroner.' Bo Fang? 'Never existed.' I asked to see the visitors' book but it was apparently destroyed in the fire. Edouard had brought it from his office for 'safekeeping'. The fire? 'Kerosene lamps lit by Erasmus and left insecure blew over in the storm, leading to total loss of the building and an irreplaceable archive. Erasmus is no longer employed by the Lodge. He had left with the other staff, including Benedict and Boniface after the tragedy; whereabouts unknown.' (I spoke to Serole Park officials. One of them could remember garbled emergency messages, which she now relates to the fire.)

It was all totally rehearsed and utterly false. If they brought a libel action against the Guardian no jury would believe them against you.

With Downside and Applebloom I nearly had a breakthrough. I interviewed them on the set of Trotter Files, both of them in costume. He was John Trotter in a dinner jacket. She was the local nurse, a part she got after the success of Roger. Like Claire and Edouard they were word-perfect, improved by thespian training. Downside was particularly good at righteous indignation that their account should be doubted. The near-breakthrough occurred *close to the end when I remarked on Applebloom's nurse's uniform and mentioned her previous career in the health service. I asked straight out if she had ever handled a severed head. For a moment she looked totally stunned, then burst into tears. She was about to say something when she was rescued by Downside, who trumpeted on about ghastly experiences of the caring professions. She recovered and I asked if any of her previous severed heads were wearing glasses. That did it. She practically collapsed and Downside terminated proceedings. She is their weak link. If it comes to court she will be destroyed.*

By way of postscript I also attempted to contact the Tanzanian coroner. He is dead. There is apparently some gang warfare in Dar es Salaam in which he was caught up. In respect of the same corpse he was required to certify accidental death by one gang and murder by the other. He attempted to certify both, which satisfied neither. Which side actually shot him is unknown.

So there it is, Arthur. I will file my copy tomorrow. I will advise the editor that we carry the whole story as a serial in five parts and that we give it maximum coverage, television leaders, the lot. I think that she will do it. Potentially the libel damages are enormous but she trusts me and my judgement and it is a bloody good story.

Yours ever, George

THE GUARDIAN

5 July 2019

Dear Arthur,

I really don't know how to say this.

Today at 9 a.m. I had a meeting with the editor, the final meeting to discuss Dump. She had Dan Wilkes ('The Money') with her and a lawyer whose name I forget. On her desk she had all my papers, notes, advice and the manuscript of Dump. She came straight to the point. 'They' had decided that publication was no longer possible. I was shocked and of course demanded to know why. She had received a letter from Claire and Edouard. It contained all manner of predictable allegations. 'You were suffering from depression, a nervous breakdown, delusions. You could not hold down your job and were bitter, etc., etc.' Everything we have heard before. Then came the strike. They said they were in possession of an email from you, apparently obtained from your Oxford computer, to which Claire has access. It was clear that you had sent the manuscript to a literary agent for publication as fiction. I demanded to see it and they showed me a redacted copy. I protested that the email said that it did not matter how the book was published, even including fiction, but then the lawyer came in. He said that it would be deadly in cross-examination, that you would have to give evidence first and that our whole case would be likely to collapse. He added, of course, that the damages would be 'eye-watering'.

So that was it. It would be possible to try other titles, the red tops, but in reality no one will touch it. I am really very sorry.

The dreaded 'send' button again. Try to put it behind you, Arthur. After all, Dump is dead. His malign presence is no more. That at least you achieved. Let us have dinner soon.

   Very best wishes,

   George

CHAPTER 33

The Times, 22 October 2019

Professor Found Dead in Oxford Home
'Depressed' wildlife expert took his own life

Dr Arthur Welbourne, the celebrated author of The Prototype
Primate, *was found dead at his home in Oxford yesterday morning.
It is thought that he took his own life some days previously. His
body was discovered in his study by neighbours, alerted after a
postman had repeatedly failed to deliver a registered letter from a
firm of solicitors. Police sources confirmed that he had apparently
climbed onto a pile of academic books, placed his neck into a
noose and kicked them from beneath him. A brief note addressed
to his wife was found on his desk.*

*Dr Welbourne became famous for his study of chimpanzees in
Serole in Tanzania with the publication of* The Prototype Primate
*in 2001. Controversially he maintained that chimpanzees, man's
closest cousins, were not a 'step on the evolutionary ladder' but
prototype humans, an experimental cul de sac from which no
further development was possible. He recently resigned his position
as Emeritus Professor of Anthropology at St John's College. The
post has been awarded to his former wife and collaborator, Claire,
herself a distinguished academic. The couple have no children. It is*

thought that their estrangement was due in part to disagreements relating to the future of primate research and conservation. This culminated with the publication of Sustainable Forestry and the Chimpanzee: A Vision for Harmony *by Claire Welbourne and Edouard Deprès. In a* Times *review Arthur Welbourne described the book as 'the ultimate betrayal'.*

Claire Welbourne is presently based at the research centre founded in her name in Serole. Recent endowments from Chinese interests have made it the world's leading institute for primate study. Speaking exclusively to The Times, *she said, 'We are all greatly saddened by the news of Arthur's death. He was a fine academic and, in his day, probably one of the best in his field. It is no secret that he had become very depressed and was unable or unwilling to adapt to new ideas and challenges. I will always fondly remember our years of research together at Serole. His last written words were addressed to me and I would rather not reveal the personal content. I am delighted that my forthcoming presentation at the Royal Geographical Society will be entitled "The Arthur Welbourne Lecture".'*

Edouard Deprès, owner and manager of the Serole Lodge, described Arthur Welbourne as 'a fine scientist who followed rigorous principles' and said, 'He will be much missed in the exciting years that lie ahead.'

Sources from St John's College declined to comment.

A full obituary of Professor Arthur Welbourne OBE will appear in The Times *on 29 October.*